THE MISSING 'GATOR OF GUMBO LIMBO

An Ecological Mystery

For the students of Norwood School,
Best wishes, —
Jean Craighead George

Jean Craighead George

HarperCollins*Publishers*

THE MISSING 'GATOR OF GUMBO LIMBO
An Ecological Mystery

Copyright © 1992 by Jean Craighead George
All rights reserved. No part of this book may be used or reproduced
in any manner whatsoever without written permission except in
the case of brief quotations embodied in critical articles and reviews.
Printed in the United States of America. For information address HarperCollins
Children's Books, a division of HarperCollins Publishers,
10 East 53rd Street, New York, NY 10022.
Published simultaneously in Canada by HarperCollins Publishers Ltd.,
Suite 2900, Hazelton Lanes, 55 Avenue Road, Toronto, Ontario, M5R 3L2.
Typography by Elynn Cohen
1 2 3 4 5 6 7 8 9 10
First Edition

Library of Congress Cataloging-in-Publication Data
George, Jean Craighead, date
    The missing 'gator of Gumbo Limbo : an ecological mystery / by Jean Craighead
George.
        p.   cm.
    Summary: Sixth-grader Liza K., one of five homeless people living in an unspoiled
forest in southern Florida, searches for a missing alligator destined for official
extermination and studies the delicate ecological balance keeping her outdoor home
beautiful.
    ISBN 0-06-020396-X. — ISBN 0-06-020397-8 (lib. bdg.)
    [1. Alligators—Fiction. 2. Wildlife conservation—Fiction.
3. Ecology—Fiction. 4. Florida—Fiction. 5. Homeless persons—Fiction.]
I. Title.
PZ7.G2933Mi 1992   91-20779
[Fic]—dc20   CIP
                                                                          AC

92 - 435

To the memory of my father,
Frank C. Craighead, Sr.,
who studied the role of the
alligator in the Everglades ecology,
and to my mother,
Carolyn J. Craighead
who, lively, alert,
and busy at 101 years of age,
takes her daily walk past the woods people's
hammock to the great horned owl's nest.

~ Contents ~

～ Foreword ～

We human beings did not weave the web of life—we are a strand in it. A hole in the web made by our cutting down a rain forest or pushing a species into extinction harms us. All life is interconnected.

We do not weave the web, but we can mend it. A group of children in Iowa planted the original prairie grasses in their yards to restore a strand of the prairie ecosystem. The people of Washington and Oregon saved a forest of old trees and the spotted owl. A family in Connecticut sowed wild lupine to save an endangered butterfly.

The web has many holes; but it has millions of human hands to fix them. Now that we know what we have done to the web, we see that our role as an intelligent animal is to mend it.

There are millions of Gumbo Limbo Holes on this earth, from a city window box or vacant lot to streams and lakes to the wilderness areas of Alaska. And there are millions of young people who know that recycling, planting, protecting, and controlling pollution is the silk that mends the web—and they are enthusiastically reconnecting the strands.

Thank you.

—J.C.G.

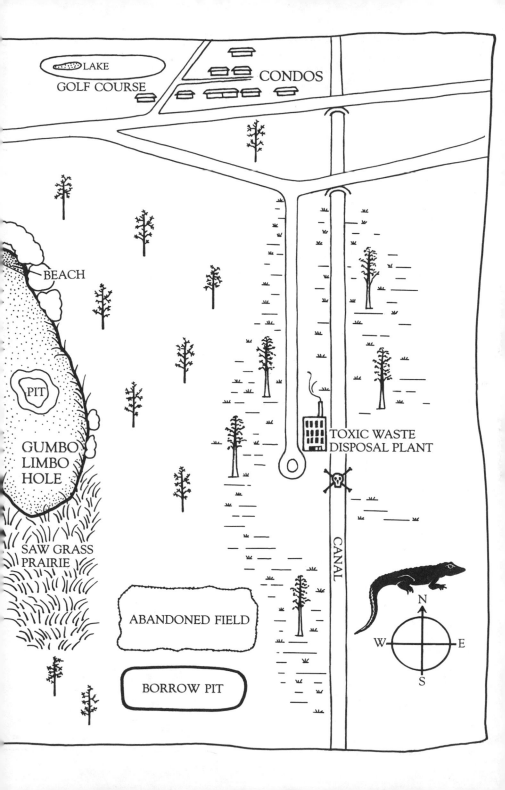

1
Missing

On a warm sun-spangled day, a reedy man in a tan cap walked into the woods. I was fishing for bass in Gumbo Limbo Hole and listening to the trade winds chime through the leaves of the royal palm. I didn't see him until he spoke.

"Missy," he said, "have you seen the big alligator that lives in this lake?"

"You mean Dajun?" I asked enthusiastically as I reeled in my line.

"I don't know what his name is," the man said.

"All I know is that he's ten feet long."

"That's got to be Dajun," I said, looking up into a sun-beaten face and keen eyes peering out from under the cap like an armadillo's under his bony armor. "Only he's twelve feet long, not ten." I checked my bait, saw it had been chewed off, and put on another shrimp. I cast far out onto the winking surface of the lake.

"Come to think of it," I said when my sinker hit bottom, "I haven't seen him for a couple of days."

That was odd. Dajun was always around. He was part of the waterscape at Gumbo Limbo Hole. He would bask on his beach in the morning and bask again in the heat of the afternoon in the cool water, his back, head, and tail exposed to the sun. The rest of the time he was watching for careless fish, turtles, birds, and beasts with only his eyes and nose above the surface of the water. Dajun was swampland royalty. I scanned the lake. He was nowhere to be seen.

"The Pest Control Department hired me," the man said. "I'm here to shoot him."

"Shoot him?" I all but shouted. "You can't do that. Alligators are protected by law."

"Not when they get over eight feet." He touched the pistol on his hip and sized me up. He took in my five feet one inches, my head of brown corkscrew curls, my freckles, and my blue eyes. He smacked his lips. "The one I'm after can eat a small girl like you in one gulp." I shrugged to say I didn't believe him.

"I know he could," he insisted. "I'm an alligator hunter. Made my living hunting these critters until they passed that law about protecting them."

"But Dajun's not eating anyone," I said.

"People over there in the condos"—he gestured toward the development on the other side of the pineland—"filed a complaint. They're afraid of him. I'm surprised to see you here. Ain't you scared?"

"Dajun's not vicious," I answered, and was about to tell him how a man named James James and I fed the big alligator the snapping turtles we caught in an underwater trap. The turtles kept Dajun fat and happy. I decided not to tell him. This man was an official. I lived in the woods right behind where we were standing. I lived there with Mom and three other people. Outsiders call us "the woods people." In Florida the weather is so nice that homeless people can camp in the woods. By nature, we all feel uncomfortable around officials. Our group had never been told to leave, but that's because nobody knew we lived in these woods. Word of the terrible Dajun kept people away. He was the dragon protecting our gate.

As unobtrusively as I could, I searched under the coco plum branches that hung out over the water. I was looking for the huge woody knots that are Dajun's eyes and nose. I couldn't find them and hoped he was on the bottom of the lake. He might well have been. The official was carrying a gun. A person who carries a gun acts aggressively. Animals sense this and disappear. Last week a policeman with a gun rounded the hole. Dajun sank and, closing the water above him without a ripple, was gone.

The official, Travis—at least that was the name embroidered on his green shirt—watched me reel in my line and cast again.

"Pretty good for a girl," he said. Such uneducated statements make Mom and me furious, but I said nothing. I didn't want to start an argument that would hold him there one minute longer than need be. I bit my tongue and cast again.

Travis went about his work. He walked around the jungly shore of Gumbo Limbo Hole as best he could. He finally stopped where the pickerelweed grew tall. There he scanned the water surface. From where he stood, he could see the entire hole or lake, whatever you prefer to call our two acres of crystal water. He could see all kinds of birds—coots, gallinules, an anhinga, and two great egrets—but not the alligator. Travis made some notes in a notebook and came back.

"Is that Dajun's sunning spot over there?" he asked. He pointed to the white gently sloping beach that the alligator had made by sliding in and out of the water.

I told him it was, but right away I was sorry I had. All this man had to do was to stand where he was long enough, and Dajun would eventually come ashore to bask in the winter sunshine. I cast again, then searched the dark lily pads for Dajun's nose. He's hard to see when he's in the pads, because his nostrils are open and dark as the leaves. He closes them when he dives. Three feet back of those nostrils would be the horny coverings around his yellow eyes. Together with his nose, they make a triangle of bumps on the top of the water. They say "alligator." Only when it's very cold does he stick just his nose out, and cold weather is rare in southern Florida.

Dajun wasn't in the lily pads.

Travis fingered his gun. Desperately I plotted.

"He might be in the cypress strand," I said, pointing to a distant grove where I had never seen him. "The herons are hunting a frog hatch in there. 'Gators like herons."

"Could be there if there's enough water," Travis said. "I'll take a look." Slowly fighting his way around dense coco plums and the stiff leaves of saw palmettos, he reached the cypress strand and disappeared.

He was gone a long time. I caught two nice bass before he returned looking discouraged, his green shirt ripped by the jungle's claws. He was also sweating.

"Find him?" I asked.

"Nah."

I made no comment, but I knew my face showed such glee that I was forced to bend my head. A disgruntled Travis walked a few steps to a log covered with resurrection ferns, the kind that wither when it's dry and revive when it rains. The ferns were withered because it was December, the dry season in Florida. They crackled when he sat down.

"There's a reward for anyone who can lead me to him," he said, handing me a card with his name and telephone number on it. "You come here often?"

"Just now and then," I said cagily.

"I guess a young lady like you could use a reward." He was looking at the holes in my shirt.

"How much is it?" I asked.

"One hundred dollars." I leaned down and tied my sneaker trying to act as if it were nothing. I hoped the other woods people wouldn't learn about this. A hundred dollars would buy Priscilla a lot of the mini gin bottles she collected. Caruso might like to have a hundred dollars, since he's a concert singer and must have opera clothes. James James wouldn't want the reward. Money doesn't mean much to him. He walks everywhere and gets his clothes from the poor people's shelter.

I was getting nervous. Dajun might surface any minute; he'd been under a long time. Also, Travis might look for Dajun in the woods, although alligators rarely, if ever, go into the woods and he must know that. But the thought of him entering for any reason at all made me bite my nails. Mom's and my home was there. He might find it and report us. We'd have to move to the shelter for the homeless. That happened to Caruso once and he never got over it.

Mom says we are not homeless. We are just on vacation until she can buy a house.

I put the official's card in my pocket.

"Sir," I said pleasantly, "do you know what time it is?"

He looked at his watch. "Five o'clock."

"Oh, wow, I've got to get home." I reeled in line, hook and sinker. "By the way, sir," I said meekly, "you say Dajun is dangerous?"

"Very dangerous," he replied. "He can kill. Seen a fellow chewed legless by one smaller than that one."

"Really?" I put on my most helpless expression. "I've seen him on the trail from time to time. Would you mind walking me to the road?"

"I'll be glad to," he replied, and took off his cap to wipe the perspiration from his forehead. He had very blue eyes, and the hair that stuck out from under his cap was sunburned a bright yellow. The hair protected by his cap was dark brown. He looked like a chocolate-covered vanilla cupcake.

"Besides," he went on, "I've been here since sunup and haven't seen even one 'gator eye. I'll post a reward notice. Someone will see him and call me." He took out a black marking pen, wrote on a sheet of notebook paper, and tacked it on the royal palm.

"Okay, fisher gal," he said. "Let's go."

I picked up my stringer of fish, my rod, and the bait box and walked behind Travis. Once we were out of the woods, we followed Gumbo Limbo Trail through low bushes and grass to the road.

"You'll be all right now," he said, smiling for the first time. "That 'gator won't get you here. Road's too hot."

"Thank you," I said, and started walking toward the condominiums.

When I heard Travis's car accelerate, I turned right around and ran back to the royal palm, tore down the reward sign, and stuffed it in my pocket. I was certain it had not been seen. I had been gone only ten minutes.

Back at my fishing spot I looked for Dajun, but still could not find him. That was most unusual. Where was he?

I did see that the turtle trap had gone off and was pleased with that. James James and I could feed Dajun the turtle and he'd be quiet for a day or so. Smiling at the thought, I cleaned the fish and carried them home for supper.

I took my long personal trail home. It winds off into the open land, where I often see butterflies on the fire plants and rabbit tobacco, then crosses through the pineland and enters the woods from the west. A few paces and it rounds a huge clump of leather fern twice as tall as I am. Then I am home.

Mom and I live in a yellow wall tent under the most beautiful live oak in Collier County. The oak is so big Mom and I, even by holding hands, cannot reach each other around the tree. Its limbs would cover a tennis court. On its branches grow gardens of orchids and the sparklerlike plants with bright flowers called "air plants" or bromeliads. Butterflies hover over the flowers and birds chase the butterflies. Lizards chase the insects. You could watch the show in this tree all day. It's a theater of horror, suspense, and romance.

Our oak is in a forest of tropical trees and bushes with names like bustic, pigeon plum, tallowwood, mastic, soapberry, and push-and-holdback. There are wild coffee trees and the edible cabbage palms. Mahogany trees, three feet in diameter, grow in the center of the woods. A black ironwood, with wood so dense it will not float, grows near our oak. The woods are called a hardwood or tropical hammock and shelter wonderful birds like the white-crowned pigeon and endangered species like the colorful tree snails. I learned all this from James James, who says our hammock is a rare thing. We may be living in the only place like it on the whole revolving planet.

The first night that Mom and I were in the woods we stretched out on our sleeping bags in the yellow tent and listened to the great horned owl call to his mate. I was very happy. The owls talked back and forth and the moonlight made leaf patterns on the tent roof. Then suddenly, I grew afraid.

"Mom," I said, my voice shaking, "is Daddy coming to live with us?"

"No, Liza K.," she answered. "No, he is not." She got up and moved her sleeping bag beside me. "Everything is going to be all right," she whispered. "He will not come here."

When we all three lived together, I did many terrible things for which my father hit me. "Come here, Liza Katherine Poole," he would shout. I knew when he called me by my full name that I had done something awful and I would tremble. When he had punished me and stormed away, I would cry and pray to be a better person. I also tried to write down what I had done, so I would never do it again. I usually couldn't remember, which made me cry even more. One night after my father had punished me very hard, and stormed out of the house, Mom came to me as she usually did. She rocked me in her arms.

"Tomorrow, Liza K.," she said, her voice very strong and sure, "you and I are going on a vacation to a beautiful place. You have done nothing wrong, my darling child. You must understand that. Do you?" I wasn't sure I did.

The next day we came to the woods.

Mom—her name is Charlotte Ann Poole—put up the wall tent she had kept from the days when she had camped with her father. She hung orchids at the door and rolled two stones side by side to make a table for her Coleman stove.

I put my butterfly jars and nets in one corner of

the tent and my fishing rod against the oak. When Mom had put our clothes in two cardboard boxes at the foot of our sleeping bags, she placed a candle on a wooden box between them. She said candles looked like glowworms in the woods and would not draw attention to our home. At sundown we sat outside the tent on stones rolled up to our orange-crate table. I shall never forget that night. The light from the setting sun turned the woods into a golden temple. "Liza K.," Mom said looking up, "we will start a new life under this beautiful tree—just you and me." She clasped her fingers together and looked around.

"My father and I lived here long ago—after my mother died." She ran her hands through her hair. "We moved back into town after he bought his shrimp boat, but we would come back here to camp and fish when the season was over. He planned to bring you here when you grew up, but he died when you were still very young." She reached over and took my hand. "He and I were peaceful here." The owl called again. "A woods is healing."

I nodded.

"You'll be pretty much on your own," she went on. "I have just taken a job waiting tables at night at the diner, and I'm going to business school in the morning. When I finish, I'll get a good job and buy a nice house." She pulled me to my feet, and we walked into the tent to get ready for bed. It was quite late when we lay down by the soft glow of the candle.

"Liza K.," Mom said when she saw I was wide awake, "maybe I'll buy that little house under the royal poinciana tree on Japonica Street, the white house with the tile patio. Remember it? It has two bedrooms, one for each of us."

I was thinking about my father. He didn't know where we were.

"Remember it, Liza K.?" she said with a lilt in her voice. She blew out the candle. "I took you there once. It has a bright-blue bathroom and a kitchen window that looks out on a papaya and a wild cinnamon tree."

I didn't remember it, possibly because I didn't care about a house as much as Mom did. I was so very peaceful in the woods in our cozy yellow tent where my father couldn't take off his belt and beat me.

2
The
Woods People

When I got back after seeing Travis off, I rolled the fish in cornmeal and put them in a pan over a low flame on the stove. Then I went back to the hole to look for Dajun. James James—his real name is James Double so everyone calls him James James—was hauling in the snapping turtle trap.

"James James," I said running to him, "an official is going to shoot Dajun."

"What?" he said, stopping his work.

"Shoot Dajun," I repeated. "He's gotten too big."

I glanced toward the glassy gumbo limbo trees to see if Priscilla was listening. She was too far away to hear us, but not too far to be seen. Through the curtain of strangler fig roots I could just see her head bent over her card table. She was writing poetry in her notebook. She writes about Dajun. *Dajun of Gumbo Limbo Hole* is the title of her epic poem.

Without a word I gave James James the reward notice. He read it, crumpled it, and stuffed it in his pocket. We looked at each other and agreed not to mention the reward to anyone, particularly Priscilla.

"I don't know what she does with all those mini gin bottles," James James said. "But whatever it is, I don't think we should encourage it with a hundred dollars." I nodded. Priscilla had several bags of these mini bottles by her table. Whenever she got her welfare check at the post office, she came home with more.

"I hope she isn't harming herself," James James murmured more to himself than to me. I didn't answer because I couldn't understand how collecting little bottles could hurt anyone, so I got to the point.

"What are we going to do about Dajun?" I asked. "We really need him to protect us from outside people."

"We'll have to get him out of Gumbo Limbo Hole for a while," he said. "Tell you what; I'll lure him into the solution pit with this turtle. Then we'll feed him so much he won't move out. When the Pest Control man thinks Dajun's dead or gone, we'll lure him back to the lake."

I liked the idea of Dajun in our solution pit. Solution pits are peculiar to limestone country, particularly in Florida. They are sinkholes that can be a few feet across or a hundred. Some are shallow and dry up in the winter dry season; others are very deep, with steep limestone walls. James James says they are made by the acid from decaying plants eating into Florida's limestone bedrock. The pit in Gumbo Limbo Hammock is about twenty feet across—a big one—and James James doesn't know how deep. It is back among the mahogany trees and surrounded by wax myrtle, water oak, and spackleberry. In the rainy season of summer it fills to within one foot of the rim. During the dry season it falls three or four feet. Lacy mosses and ferns grow down its walls.

One fern, the Venus'-hair fern, grows nowhere else in the world but on the walls of Florida solution pits.

Dajun would like it. I think all beasts know beauty when they see it; certainly Dajun likes the pretty lily pads and his pure white sandy beach. Since I spend a lot of time around the pit looking for caterpillars and butterflies, I found it exciting to think of having Dajun there to talk to.

We woods people get our drinking and bath water from the solution pit. James James tests it from time to time. It is as pure as sunshine, he says. The water comes from the Tamiami aquifer, a layer of porous rock below many layers of clay and limestone. The layers are mostly old ocean beds that stretch from where we are in La Playa all the way to Georgia. The aquifer gets its water from the rain. It percolates down from layer to layer and then, like all water, it moves downhill seeking the sea. It moves very slowly. James James says the water in our solution pit could have fallen as rain in Georgia ten thousand years ago. It tastes wonderful and feels silky. Mom and I put buckets of pit water out in the sun to heat up, then we wash with soapberries and jump in down at the orange-crate table and asked if we had any mini gin bottles. Mom looked at her scornfully.

"Don't be shocked," James James had said when he saw Mom's face. "That's Priscilla's way of welcoming you to the woods."

"Thank you very much," Mom said, extending her hand to Priscilla and smiling her wide smile that perks up everyone.

"And," James James went on, "I welcome you, too." I did not know at the time how special those greetings were. I would learn later that woods people don't like outsiders. At that time I knew only that they were nice people and I liked them. No one asked us why we were there. I guess they didn't have to. Mom told me, after they had left, that she had gone to the woods before she moved us there to see if it was as isolated as she remembered. She had run into James James baiting his turtle trap.

"You'll be just fine here," he had assured her after they had talked a bit. "Old Dajun the dragon keeps everyone away, and I'll make sure your daughter does her homework."

He did far more than that. He made sure I got

up in time to walk the half mile to school, and he arranged leaf quizzes on the orange crate when I came home at four. There are two thousand plants in southern Florida, and I think he's made me learn four hundred. The ones I like best are the ones that fix bellyaches and mosquito bites.

But back to James James and the turtle. He gave up trying to lure Dajun with it and dragged it up on shore. He looked very perplexed and discouraged.

"Why don't you call Dajun?" I asked. "He always comes when you call."

"We usually have to see each other to have that work," he said. "But I'll give it a try." He cupped his hands around his mouth.

"GUGH UGH UGH UGH, UGHAAAAAR-RRRRRRRRR," he roared in the manner of the bull alligator. We waited; there was no response. The egrets went on preening their feathers and the pintail ducks swam peacefully in and out of the reeds to say that there was no bull alligator near them.

"Where the heck can he be?" James James asked.

"Could he be dead?" I ventured.

"No," he replied. "The scavengers would be after him. We'd see vultures in the air, turtles in the

Gumbo Limbo Hole to rinse.

Since the solution pit is quite far from Gumbo Limbo Hole, I asked James James how he was going to get Dajun to follow him there.

"He'll follow if he's hungry enough," he answered. "Tiger Wind, my Seminole Indian friend, has twelve alligators in a pen in his village. When they're hungry, they'll follow him a quarter of a mile to his chickee—his house of poles with a palm leaf roof. When they're not, they won't move."

"Dajun had better be hungry," I said. "Travis is coming back tomorrow."

James James took the drowned turtle with its pointed nose and bear-trap jaws out of the trap and tied a rope around its neck. Then he walked to the shore of Gumbo Limbo Hole looking for Dajun. Two egrets in a coco plum preened their snowy white feathers and an anhinga swam with its body under water and its head and long neck above the surface like a snake. Sometimes they are called snake birds.

"No signs of Dajun," James James said, his brown eyes narrowing as he scanned the glassy surface. "As a matter of fact," he went on, "I haven't see him for several days. How long has this official been hunting him?"

"He didn't tell me."

James James threw the turtle far out into the water and jerked the rope to make the creature look alive. No Dajun swirled up to take it as he usually did.

James James, who likes just about everything that's alive, even bedbugs, doesn't like snapping turtles. They pull little ducklings under the water, then drown and eat them. Dajun does too, but he serves a good purpose, James James says. He not only keeps people out of the woods, he weeds the lake so the fish can multiply and feed the birds and mammals and us. Dajun does a professional job when it comes to removing the weeds. He crosses Gumbo Limbo Hole like a bulldozer. He shoves water plants before him and then up on shore. The water twinkles clear wherever he has plowed.

James James threw the turtle out again and slowly dragged it in. James James moves slowly, he once told me, so he can savor being alive. When he returned from the Vietnam War, he didn't want to go to work ever again. He wanted to look and smell and listen, so he set out across the United States, sleeping wherever he was when the sun went down. He had studied wildlife biology and geology in college and knew the whereabouts of the beautiful places on earth. After the war he set out to find them—the sequoia forests of California, the alpine tundras of Wyoming, and the tall grass prairies of Kansas. One day he came upon Gumbo Limbo Hammock. It lies on the eastern outskirts of La Playa, a winter resort on the tip of the Florida peninsula on the Gulf of Mexico. He told me how he walked into it one day, smelled, saw, listened, and stayed.

In Gumbo Limbo Hammock, James James fashioned what he called The Niche. A niche, he told me, is an ecological term for a place an individual or species occupies in a community of plants and animals.

"And that individual or species has a role to play in the community," he said.

"What is yours?" I asked.

"I don't know yet," he answered very softly, and looked up at the canopy of the hammock.

The Niche is under, within, and up in a huge banyan tree. The air roots of the tree come down to the earth and grow like a forest. You squeeze between them into rooms and dens. Some of these James James has roofed with palm thatch so they won't leak when it rains. His bed is ten or twelve feet up in the tree in a string hammock. The mosquitoes that live in the woods fly no higher than nine feet, so they never bite James James when he's in his bed. His chairs are pillows, all kinds of discarded pillows he's found in the old and wealthy part of town. He calls The Niche his university, and it must be. He is always learning something there.

After James James settled down in Gumbo Limbo Hammock, he wandered out to see the town pier in the gulf. There he met Caruso. He was homeless, so James James invited him to Gumbo Limbo Hammock. Caruso "nested" under the mahogany tree. His real name is Joe Carlo, and he is a famous opera singer. About a month after Caruso had made his home, he met Priscilla. She followed him home and put down her bags among the gumbo limbos and settled in. A year ago Mom and I arrived and put up our tent under the oak. James James came over to admire it, Caruso walked all around it, and Priscilla sat down at the orange-crate table and asked if we had any mini gin bottles. Mom looked at her scornfully.

"Don't be shocked," James James had said when he saw Mom's face. "That's Priscilla's way of welcoming you to the woods."

"Thank you very much," Mom said, extending her hand to Priscilla and smiling her wide smile that perks up everyone.

"And," James James went on, "I welcome you, too." I did not know at the time how special those greetings were. I would learn later that woods people don't like outsiders. At that time I knew only that they were nice people and I liked them. No one asked us why we were there. I guess they didn't have to. Mom told me, after they had left, that she had gone to the woods before she moved us there to see if it was as isolated as she remembered. She had run into James James baiting his turtle trap.

"You'll be just fine here," he had assured her after they had talked a bit. "Old Dajun the dragon keeps everyone away, and I'll make sure your daughter does her homework."

He did far more than that. He made sure I got

up in time to walk the half mile to school, and he arranged leaf quizzes on the orange crate when I came home at four. There are two thousand plants in southern Florida, and I think he's made me learn four hundred. The ones I like best are the ones that fix bellyaches and mosquito bites.

But back to James James and the turtle. He gave up trying to lure Dajun with it and dragged it up on shore. He looked very perplexed and discouraged.

"Why don't you call Dajun?" I asked. "He always comes when you call."

"We usually have to see each other to have that work," he said. "But I'll give it a try." He cupped his hands around his mouth.

"GUGH UGH UGH UGH, UGHAAAAAR-RRRRRRRRR," he roared in the manner of the bull alligator. We waited; there was no response. The egrets went on preening their feathers and the pintail ducks swam peacefully in and out of the reeds to say that there was no bull alligator near them.

"Where the heck can he be?" James James asked.

"Could he be dead?" I ventured.

"No," he replied. "The scavengers would be after him. We'd see vultures in the air, turtles in the water. A twelve-foot carcass would cause a lot of activity."

"Maybe he left," I said.

"Doubt it," James James replied. "The only thing that would cause him to leave would be lack of food. Gumbo Limbo Hole is a zoo-arium."

"He might be hunting a mate," I said.

"Wrong season."

"Well, we've got to find him before Travis does," I said. "So what do we do?"

"I'll circle the hole," he answered. "Maybe I can find his tracks or some clue to his whereabouts. You stay here and watch for him."

He put the turtle back in the trap so the vultures and raccoons wouldn't get it, washed his hands in the clear blue water, and dried them on his hair.

James James is tall and bony with black hair, a long slim nose, and ruddy cheeks. His blue jeans are frayed but he always wears nice clean shirts. Mom and I wonder how he washes them. We never see him carrying laundry over to the Laundromat like we do. I think he uses the soapy bark of the slippery elm tree and washes his clothes in the cypress swamp. Mom thinks he wears them to the pier and washes them under the outdoor showers. Then he wears them home, drying them as he walks.

James James threaded among the jungle plants as slowly and gracefully as an egret. His head moved from side to side as he searched the waterscape.

While he scouted, I stood on the bank trying to think like a nature detective. Alligators have lungs and must surface for air. I would watch for bubbles. Bubbles are alligator footprints, so to speak. They rise and lie on the surface like tracks. I couldn't see any bubbles and sat down to watch the birds gathering for the evening. They would betray the old dragon with their chatter and screams if he were in the bushes along the edge of the water. The birds were calm, their voices throaty and conversational.

Presently Caruso came up the trail dressed for a concert in his black suit and white shirt. He was wearing his top hat with the red feather in it. He told James James he found the feather in Gumbo Limbo Hammock, but he and I didn't believe it. It's a tail feather and there are no birds with bright-red tails in Florida. The sun struck the feather, and it fairly glowed as the old man approached.

"Caruso," I said, "the officials are going to shoot Dajun."

"That's horrible," he exclaimed, throwing back his coat and sticking his thumbs in his suspenders. "They can't do that. He's our dragon, our guardian, our good friend."

"He'll be all right," I said, seeing how perturbed he was. "James James is going to hide him."

"Hide him?"

"He'll lure him into the solution pit," I said. Caruso thought about that, nodded, and pursed his lips.

"Clever, that James James," he said.

"Except we can't find Dajun. No one has seen him for a while. Have you?"

"Come to think of it, no," he answered, and walked to the water to have a look. Suddenly I remembered the fish that I had left cooking on the stove. "Try to find Dajun," I called, and ran home.

Mom had removed the fish and was heating up the soup leftovers the owner of the diner gave her. She brings the leftovers home every day, often with biscuits and butter.

I was glad to see the fish weren't burned, then turned to Mom. "An official's going to kill Dajun!"

"Oh, no," she said. "He can't do that. Dajun protects us from outside people."

"And Priscilla writes poems about him," I added. "She needs him for inspiration."

"She writes poetry?" Mom took off the jacket she wears for her business school. "Is it any good?"

"I've never seen any of her poetry, but she ought to be good at it. She was once an editor for a magazine in New York."

"She was? What on earth is she doing here?" Mom asked.

"Well . . ." I answered carefully because I had never read her poems, just talked to her about them. "Her poetry doesn't sell very well, so she has to live frugally." I sat down on my limestone seat. "But that's not the real reason she lives in the woods. She's afraid to be indoors. She can't stand walls around her." I looked at Mom. I needed her to be very honest with me. Some of the kids at school who had seen Priscilla in town said she was crazy. "Is that crazy, Mom?"

"No," she answered thoughtfully. "Some people need to be free and unfettered." She looked up at the magnificent oak as if she was speaking for herself. We sat down at the orange crate and began eating our soup and fish.

"Liza K.," she said when we were almost done, "Priscilla has been hurt very deeply. She once lived in a beautiful house. She showed me a picture of it. I asked her why she had left such a lovely place, and she said that the walls were closing in on her, her house getting smaller and smaller. She became very frightened and took a bus to see a relative in Florida. She never looked her relative up. Instead she lived on and under the La Playa pier. The police would urge her to move on, but she would come back to the pier when they let her alone. Then she met Caruso, and he recommended the privacy of Gumbo Limbo Hammock."

"She must be happy here," I said, speaking for myself.

"I don't know about that," Mom answered slowly. "But, perhaps she is, if she writes poetry."

"Why does she collect mini gin bottles?" I asked this gingerly, because I knew Priscilla's minis were disturbing to Mom.

"I've never asked her," she answered evasively, but then everyone was evasive about the minis around me. I don't think they wanted me to know what Priscilla did with them.

"But Liza K.," she said, getting to her feet, "I like her very much. She's so very gentle." As I scraped my bowl clean, Mom ladled out a third cup of soup.

"You'd better take Priscilla her soup before it gets dark," she said. ". . . And give her my love."

Priscilla lived in the grove of handsome gumbo limbo trees with their red bark and silver-green leaves. Her bed was a wicker love seat someone had thrown away, and her office, as she called it, was a card table under a thatched palm roof James James had built for her. She was writing when I walked up.

"Good evening, Liza K.," she said, closing her notebook and glancing at the soup. "Oh, dear. You've gone to such trouble and I'm not hungry at all."

"Well, I'll just put it on the stump," I said. "Maybe you'll be hungry later, or you can give it to the raccoons."

"That's a lovely idea," she said.

Every night we went through this routine, and every night she ate the soup as soon as I turned my back and started home.

"An official's going to kill Dajun," I said.

Priscilla's fingers clutched the edges of the table and she rose to her feet.

"No. Please tell him no." The color had drained from her face. "People will come in here when he's dead and take me away."

"No they won't, Priscilla," I said with great confidence. "James James, Caruso, and I are going to save him."

"You must," she whispered. "I need to know he's there."

"We have a plan," I went on. "He'll be safe tomorrow." She looked at me without much conviction.

"Really," I said. She smiled pathetically and picked up her soup. For the first time she ate it while I was still there.

Mom called me, and after reassuring Priscilla again, I ran home through the woods. I guess I needn't have worried that Priscilla would have wanted the one-hundred-dollar reward for Dajun. She loved him as much as I did.

I really loved Priscilla too. She was a poet, and poets are very special people. They give words to the thoughts we cannot express ourselves.

3

The Pit
and the Lake
and the Hole

The next morning was the beginning of winter vacation. I was up before the great horned owl came home from hunting and before the little lizards called anoles were warm enough to move and run. It was the hour when spiderwebs gathered dew and butterflies hung upside down at the tips of leaves waiting for the sun. The air was damp and heavy to breathe.

It was so early, Mom would not be leaving the diner for two hours. I picked an orange from a wild orange tree the Spaniards had left behind and took a biscuit from the tin bread box. The orange was deep gray, the biscuit pale gray for it was still night.

When I reached Gumbo Limbo Hole, the orange was orange and the biscuit was tan. The stripes on my shirt had changed from many grays to many reds. The sun had risen and I could see color again.

The sun comes up swiftly over southern Florida. On this day there was darkness, then pink light; then—pop—a red-hot penny of a sun was sitting on the horizon. With that a colorful Gumbo Limbo Hammock materialized. Green palm leaves pranced like tethered ponies in the morning breeze. Yellow flowers rustled.

I could also see Dajun's beach where he came ashore during the day to bask in the sun. He wasn't there. I looked at his night camp which, at this time of year, was in the deep water of the hole. In winter this water is warmer than the night air. Dajun, like all reptiles, is cold-blooded. He cannot manufacture heat, as humans do. Instead, he regulates his temperature by moving from the water to the land and back to the water, depending on which will keep his temperature normal. He is a sunshine animal, hunting and bulldozing and basking on his beach by day. When he gets too hot, he goes into the water to cool off. In the hot afternoons he often regulates his temperature by floating at the surface. The sun warms his back and the water cools his belly and feet. At night, when the air is colder than the water, he seeks out deep holes for warmth.

As I stood there, eyes on Dajun's beach, Travis materialized in the sunlight. I backed slowly into the alligator flags, a tall plant that grows around alligator holes. Hidden among the flaglike leaves I watched. If Travis had seen me that morning, he would certainly have wondered about me. Why would I come back today after being so scared last night?

The official turned his head slowly surveying the lake, and then eased himself backward into the dense willows. Pulling branches over and around himself, he sat down, took out his pistol, and lifted his binoculars. My heart thumped so loudly I could hear it. His gun was aimed at the saw grass prairie at the far end of the lake. During the day Dajun often hunts snakes and muskrats in these grasses that grow in the knee-deep water. My only thought was to scare the old dragon into hiding.

I crept out of the flags and, dropping to all fours, scuttled into the woods like a raccoon. Near the banyan tree I ran into James James. Getting to my feet, I put my finger over my lips and pointed to Dajun's beach.

"James James," I whispered, "Travis has his gun aimed at Dajun in the saw grass prairie. I'm going there to throw rocks at him and scare him away."

"Don't bother," he answered. "I've just come from there. He's not in the prairie."

"He's not?" I said in gleeful surprise. "Then where is he? He's not in Gumbo Limbo Hole or on his beach."

"I don't know." James James rubbed his temple with the tip of his forefinger. "But we can't look for him while that official is there on his beach."

"Think, James James," I said pleadingly. "Think."

"Okay, you climb the oak tree. There's a large limb at the top with a great view. Look for Dajun while I join Travis. I'll walk in to him from the north as if I was coming from the condos. I'll tell him I saw his reward notice. Then I'll say the big 'gator is in the lake on the golf course. I'll take him there and leave him." He smiled puckishly. "That'll give us time to get Dajun into the solution pit when he comes out to bask on his beach."

James James started off. He had walked about ten steps when he stopped and came quietly back.

"If you see Travis leave the beach before I reach him," he whispered, "call like a great horned owl. One hoot means he's going toward Gumbo Limbo Trail, two owl hoots mean he's going to the saw grass prairie. Either way, I'll cut over and meet up with him."

"Got it," I said.

Before climbing the tree, I went to the solution pit. I wanted to be sure Dajun had not gone there on his own. I would know if he had. He flattens and tramples the plants when he walks.

The plants were perky and unsmashed. Nevertheless, I checked the water. It was dark and clear. Little fish swam vigorously. They come into the solution pits through the holes in the limestone when the winter sun dries up the wet prairies and swamps. A snake crossed the water and a frog leaped in and disappeared. Behind him came a weasel, who stopped and sat up on his haunches. He looked at me unafraid; but there was no Dajun.

Satisfied on that point, I climbed the oak using our orange crate to reach the first limb. After that, the branches provided a staircase to the top of the tree.

Poking my head through the leafy canopy, I looked out on our world. I was an eagle surveying my home. I could see my enemy, Travis. He was still in the willows behind Dajun's beach. Surrounding my hammock on three sides was pineland. On the fourth side was the saw grass prairie, where Travis thought Dajun was lurking. The prairie was surrounded by a cypress swamp. Beyond the cypress swamp was an abandoned tomato field. Still farther on in the pink haze of morning I could see Big Cypress National Preserve. It was gray because the leaves of the trees fall off in winter. I looked north to the condo village and a canal. The canal was built to drain a cypress swamp to the north so that Silver City, a new retirement town, could be built. The water drains into Chokoloskee Bay.

To the south I could see the highway to Miami cutting through cypress forests and the saw grass prairies. The mangrove swamps lay beyond the highway, and beyond the mangrove swamps the beautiful blue Chokoloskee Bay stretched all the way to the sky.

To the west the tall buildings of the County Government Center jutted above the mist that hid the sunshine town of La Playa on the Gulf of Mexico.

Hardly did I have time to absorb the details of my kingdom when I saw Mom coming down the road. She was on her way home from the diner to change into her business school clothes. She turned onto Gumbo Limbo Trail, and I sucked in my breath. Travis could see her when she reached the royal palm. The trail went along the edge of the lake at that point, and anyone walking it would be seen from Dajun's beach. Travis might catch up with her and find our home. I searched my brain for a way to turn her back.

Fortunately, James James arrived on Dajun's beach. Travis lowered his binoculars and came out of the willows to speak to him. They talked and pointed. Travis looked animated. Then James James gestured in the direction of the golf course, and Travis nodded. He followed James James toward Gumbo Limbo Trail. They would run smack into Mom coming home.

James James and I had not agreed what I should hoot if one of the woods people appeared, but I gave one hoot anyway. It did mean Gumbo Limbo Trail. Since James James was with Travis, maybe he'd conclude something was wrong with Gumbo Limbo Trail and change his course. He did. He turned right around and headed for the Prairie Trail, scratching his head as he made some explanation to Travis. There is something about living in the woods that makes it possible for people to use other languages.

I blew out a long breath as Mom walked under the royal palm in plain view of the beach that James James and Travis had left only a second ago.

I stayed in the treetop. My eagle's-eye view was giving me new insights into Dajun's world. Gumbo Limbo Hammock is circular. The Hole, which is the size of a football field, is its northern border. The solution pit is almost in the center of the hammock, as if the trees had grown out around it—which they had, James James said. The hammock trees, which are hardwoods, grow on the highest land in the county, the rocky hammock land. Hammocks are only three or four feet higher than the pinelands that surround them. On yet lower land the cypress trees grow, and on the lowest land the saw grass takes over. I had been told this last year in my environmental studies class, but not until I looked down from the tree did I see that elevation does indeed determine which plants grow where. There before me was my class lesson—hardwoods on high land, pines lower, cypress lower, and saw grass so low it is in water most of the year. Dajun was a citizen of the lowlands. I could see where I had to look for him—in the cypress swamps, the wet saw grass prairie, and holes and pits and canals.

Still I didn't come down. I kept looking at Dajun's home—Gumbo Limbo Hole. James James and I never know whether Gumbo Limbo Hole is a solution pit or a lake. Florida lakes are gently sloping and lined with clay. Solution pits are steep sided and rocky. From where I sat, I now saw that Gumbo Limbo Hole was both. Its clay edges sloped gently, which made it a lake, but its center was a deep rocky pit or a solution hole. The combination was ringing bells in my head, but I couldn't find a door to open that would lead me to the answer.

One door did open to me up there. It was the one that let me see what my teacher meant when she said a hammock is an island in the woods. That's exactly what it is. Our hammock floats in a sea of pine trees. It is also a greenhouse, as we woods people and the birds and animals know. The air within is warmer in winter and cooler in summer than the outside air. A dense ever-green canopy of leaves keeps the temperature constant. We have our own furnace, air conditioner, and humidifier. More bells were ringing in my head. Alligators have to regulate their body temperature by moving in and out of the water, shade, and sun. Hammocks regulate temperature, too— think, Liza K., think. Nature was telling me where Dajun was, if only I could hear her voice.

And suddenly I thought I did. My eyes fell on the large steel drainpipe that lay under the condo road. These culverts are built all over south Florida to carry off forty to sixty-five inches of rain per year.

"Alligator hideout," I shouted gleefully. "Dajun's in that culvert." Alligators dig caves in the limestone at the edges of their water holes where the females hide their hatchlings so beasts and birds won't eat them. A culvert was a ready-made alligator cave, and the one I was looking at carried water from the condo side of the road to our side and on down to the bay. Dajun could easily have walked from Gumbo Limbo Hole's saw grass prairie to the cypress swamp, to the slough, and up it to the culvert. All those waterways were connected.

I had put my foot on a lower limb to hurry down and find him when the sun struck Gumbo Limbo Hole. It shone like a blue star in a green sky of trees. I stopped where I was and stepped back up. So clear was the water that I could see to the very bottom of both the lake and the pit, which together are Gumbo Limbo Hole. I searched for Dajun. I could see garfish and turtles and that big bass I had been trying to catch. Frogs swam toward the shade of the trees. An otter spiraled into the emerald-green pit and came up with a fish. But I did not see Dajun. He was absolutely not in Gumbo Limbo Hole. Of this I was certain.

Another look confirmed this. A dark area of

blue-green algae grew near the royal palm. Green alga is good, blue-green is not. We had learned this in school. Green alga grows under water on all objects that the sunlight can reach. It is food for the microscopic animals, which are food for larger animals. The green alga cleans the water, making it gemlike and clear. You can grow green alga by putting a glass of plain tap water in the sun for several days.

Blue-green alga, on the other hand, is an announcer of doom. It says the water is polluted with phosphorus and nitrogen from septic tanks, farms, lawns, and road runoff. That day it also said to me that there was no Dajun. If he was there, he would have bulldozed that clump of blue-green algae to shore. It suffocates the fish and turtles he lives on. Somehow he knows this and weeds it out.

Although both kinds of alga are green, they are easy to identify. The blue green is darker and is thick and stringy. It grows in blobs and clumps and quickly fills the water. The green is just a pretty bloom on underwater rocks, sticks, and leaves.

Convinced that Dajun was hiding from the

hunter in that big culvert, I started down again. I also reasoned that he was hunting somewhere else or he would have cleaned up the blue-green algae in Gumbo Limbo Hole. I stepped downward limb by limb.

Three limbs below I realized how much I missed that alligator. He made Gumbo Limbo Hole special. I remembered him lying on his beach without twitching an eye. I remembered him leaping straight up in the air like a dolphin to catch a heron on a limb. My days after school would be dull without Dajun. He was a substitute for the friends I could not bring home. Gumbo Limbo Hole would miss him, too. Weeds would fill it, and blue-green algae would thicken the water to the consistency of gravy.

I was feeling sorry for myself and the woods people when I saw Priscilla below. She had a mini gin bottle in each hand and was pushing around the coco plums into the pine forest. I leaned far out. At least I would learn why she collected those bottles.

Priscilla disappeared behind a large clump of saw palmetto. I waited, but she did not reappear.

Down on the ground Mom began humming as

she fixed breakfast before going off to her school. The smell of bacon hastened me earthward. I even passed by a beautiful zebra butterfly without stopping. I dropped onto our patio.

"Surprise," I said, startling Mom.

"Where have you been?" she snapped. "I was worried about you."

"Looking for Dajun."

"In a tree?"

"I can see our whole world from up there," I said. "The Hole, the pines, the canals, the trails—and you coming home." I sat down on my rock. "And in case you don't know it," I added sassily, "I saved you from danger."

She pinched my cheek. Her brown eyes were surrounded with smile lines. "My brave darling," she said with the same sassiness I had given her. "Was a coconut about to fall on my head?"

"No, an official was about to find you." Her eyes widened and her mouth opened ever so slightly. Mom is tall and thin with brown curly hair like mine. When she is worried, she wrinkles and shrinks. She looked very worried and small.

"You *did* save me," she said. "He can't take us away now. I'm so close to finishing my course."

She walked to the stove and turned over the bacon. Then she spun around and, shaking her head to rid it of worry, smiled brightly at me.

"The diner needs a new manager," she said. "I applied for the job today. It pays very well, Liza K., very, very well." Her lips parted, her face grew soft and smooth, and she seemed to be looking out at the little white house on Japonica Street.

James James came around the leather fern and hailed us with a big grin. Travis was not with him. He was, I imagined, walking around the lake on the golf course, weaving in and out among golfers, stopping for their shots, and looking futilely for Dajun.

"It's going to take Travis a long time to get around that lake," James James said. "There's a tournament this morning and the place is mobbed."

"Have some bacon," I said gleefully.

"I think we should get going," he answered, taking a crisp strip and sitting down. "We have to find him soon—*and* catch him."

"You don't have to hurry," I said. "I know where he is." I served myself a cup of oatmeal and began spooning it down. I had been up since five and was very hungry.

"Where is he, for heaven's sake?" Mom asked impatiently.

"In a culvert."

"Aha," she said, cocking her head as if that could be just where he was. "Have some oatmeal, James James, and make yourself at home. I've got to go or I'll be late for class." James James arose and saw her to the door, so to speak. At least, that's what his motions said, as he walked her out from under the oak and with a low sweep of his arm pointed her on her way. At times he can be very polite.

Mom's feet fairly skipped as she went through the woods, that's how much she wanted that job. As for me, I both did and didn't want her to get it.

James James sat down at the crate and ate slowly, savoring each bite as he savors walking, looking, and listening.

4
Water Clues

When breakfast was over, James James actually ran behind me all the way to the culvert. No relishing the scent of bay cedar and silverbell, no indulging in bird song or lizard watching. We ran full out down Gumbo Limbo Trail, past the butterfly field, and stopped at the culvert.

We splashed into the water and, bending down, peered into the four-foot-high culvert.

"He's not here," I said with great disappointment. "He's not here."

I couldn't believe it. Putting my hands on the bottom of the flow, I all-foured it through the culvert, splashing and soaking myself as I went. On the other side I looked around, then all-foured it back to James James.

"He's not here." I sat down on the bank and dropped my head in my hands. James James patted my shoulder.

"I'm going to the canal to see if that living dinosaur moved over there. Want to come?"

"I'll stay here," I answered. I was too discouraged to move.

"The culvert was good thinking," he said. "You're on the right track." He climbed the bank and disappeared down the road.

I stared into the water not seeing anything, just thinking how empty I felt. I had been so certain I had found our dragon and that he would soon again make our hammock safe for the woods people. Gradually my eyes came into focus. Before me swam a mere handful of tiny mosquito fish called gambusia, but there should have been thousands. These little fish eat nothing but mosquito larvae.

James James told me that gambusia, together

with the dragonflies, once kept the mosquitoes under control in southern Florida. But as swamps were drained for farms, houses, and roads, the little gambusia died off. The mosquito larvae hatched by the billions. Not even the dragonflies could control them. The county had to spray pesticides from airplanes to kill the mosquitoes, and the good insects died with the pests: the dragonflies died with the mosquitoes.

Since Gumbo Limbo Hammock is out of the spray zone, our mosquitoes are under control. The dragonflies speed through the trees like squadrons of little bombers, catching and eating their prey. Whenever I can, I walk behind them in their mosquitoless wake. I also picked my fishing spot on Gumbo Limbo Hole because it is protected by mosquito fish.

Concern for the little fish got me going again, and I four-legged it back through the culvert to see what might have killed them. When I stood up and looked around, it was very apparent. The water that ran into the culvert came from the direction of the condos and airport, which are sprayed with pesticides twice a week in the summer. The rain washes the pesticides to the drainage ditches and through the culverts, including the one where I stood. The chemicals collect in the still pools and settle on the green algae. The little fish eat the algae and die. And that is not the end. While up in the tree I had seen that the water from the culvert flowed into the cypress swamp and its slough. That meant that the pesticides were being washed into the cypress swamp. The little fish would eat the pesticides, the sunfish would eat the little fish, and the big fish, turtles, and birds would eat the sunfish. Then Dajun would eat the big fish, turtles, and birds.

Our dragon might be, if not dead, dying of a strong dose of toxic chemicals.

I was not feeling very happy when James James returned.

"Dajun is absolutely not in the canal," he said. "That new pest weed, hydrilla, is solid from shore to shore and as far up and down the canal as I can see. Even our reptilian bulldozer friend couldn't plow that weed jam." He rubbed the several days of whisker growth on his chin.

"I'm worried about that hydrilla getting a start in Gumbo Limbo Hole," he said. "It's a terrible weed."

"But it's so far away," I said.

"Birds can carry it in on their feet and even in their droppings. It's almost impossible to kill, because it has a network of roots that produce bulbs or corms by the thousands. If you kill the leafy top with a weed killer, the corms come up the next day. And one stalk can grow three quarters of an inch a day. Hydrilla suffocates the big fish and stunts the little fish. We'll starve if it gets going in Gumbo Limbo Hole. We've got to find Dajun and save him and the Hole."

"Now, where do we look?" I asked.

"He has to be somewhere." James James ran his fingers through his hair. "He didn't grow wings and fly away. A twelve-foot alligator wouldn't leave our hole and wetlands unless there was a drought and he was starving to death."

"Which he is not, thanks to the Gumbo Limbo fish and your turtle trap," I said.

We sat down to decide what to do next. A snowy egret alighted near us and walked gracefully among the reeds, his white plumes falling like lace down his long neck. He stopped, one foot lifted. His neck cricked. Like swift lightning he whipped it out and caught a fish. With a twist he tossed it in the air and swallowed it headfirst. We laughed in admiration. The egret stalked on.

"Well, *he* likes little stunted fish," said James James. "Hydrilla might do him some good." He leaned back in the grass and looked up at the small white clouds gathering like scattered sheep in the morning sky.

"Do you think a poacher might have gotten Dajun at night with a flashlight?" James James asked in such a low voice, he seemed to be talking to himself.

"No," I answered.

"I know it." He laughed. "It would be hard to poach a twelve-foot alligator in this hammock. Too many woods people watching. Just grabbing at stars." He rolled up to a sitting position. "Then where is he? We've looked everywhere."

"Not everywhere," I said.

"Where else?"

"Under us." I patted the earth. "This limestone we're sitting on is full of tunnels and caverns. Maybe he crawled into one of them."

"Why would he do that? He needs sunshine and fish."

"Scared. He knows about guns. I saw him hide

from a policeman."

"He did?" James James broke off a reed and chewed on it. "You're getting warm, Liza K.," he said. "Any alligator as big and old as Dajun must have been shot at many times during his life. He's hunter wise. And you're right, he's hiding."

"But he can't hide forever," I said. "He has to eat, and you know what that means. He'll catch something, then thrash and swirl and turn and beat the water with his tail until Travis hears him and shoots him."

"True," James James said. "We've got to get him into the solution pit."

"But first we've got to find him, " I said limply.

We both thought.

"I've got an idea," I said. "Our class went to the County Government Center last year. They had maps of the natural resources of the county; the swamps, hardwood and cypress forests, wet prairies, brackish marshes, and even the mangrove swamps."

"Mangrove swamp," said James James, taking the reed from his mouth. "Aha, if he got to a mangrove swamp, he's safe. Nothing but an alligator with his suit of armor can get through those entwined trunks and walking roots." He pulled me to my feet.

"A map *is* a good idea," he said. "We can trace the sloughs and wetlands and see if he might have gotten to safety in the mangrove swamp on the other side of the highway."

"How could he cross? The traffic's awful."

"Through the culverts." James James said. "You pointed that out."

"If the map has Gumbo Limbo Hammock on it," I said, enthusiastic once more, "it'll show caves and tunnels where Dajun might hide." I didn't believe for a minute he had gone to the mangrove swamps.

"You go to the center and get a map," James James said. "And I'll wait on Dajun's beach for Travis. I want to take him to another lake. We need more time."

Since I was on vacation, I wasn't dressed for visiting the Government Center and told James James I was going home to change.

We started off with James James leading the way down Gumbo Limbo Trail. Suddenly he stopped and pointed over the trees. About fifty vultures were circling the cypress ridge beyond the pineland.

"Something real big is dead," he said.

"Dajun?" I asked with concern.

"Could be," he answered. "Let's check it out."

We ran, scaring up a beautiful blue butterfly. Like a chip of dusty sky the fairy creature flitted to the flower of a Spanish needle and sipped nectar.

"A Miami blue," I said.

"I thought they were rare," James James remarked.

"Really?" I said. "I see a lot of them here."

"Hmmm," James James mused. We slowed down for James James to look across the butterfly field.

"There are all kinds of butterflies in the hammock," I went on. "Some of them are on the endangered animal list, the butterfly book says."

"Hmmm. Know your butterflies, do you?"

"Pretty well. I like to collect caterpillars and keep them until they hatch. Ever see a butterfly emerge?"

"As a matter of fact I have. That's how I lost my first job. I was three hours late because I was watching a drab brown bag turn into a glorious tiger swallowtail. I was fired." He sighed. "But I had seen a fantasy as miraculous as a pumpkin turning into a coach."

We ran again, crossed through the hammock taking bearings on the vultures as best we could, and entered the pine forest. The cat's claw and saw palmettos tore at our clothes as we worked our way through that mean land; and then we were in the cypress forest. We sank up to our knees in muck as we rounded the flanges of huge old trees. The air roots of the strangler figs held us to a crawl. I've always wondered how the Spanish explorer, Ponce de León and his men strode around Florida in all that armor—or even without it.

After about an hour we came to the canal where the vultures were congregating.

"The kill's a lot bigger than Dajun," James James said as we approached.

Pushing back willow limbs, we climbed the canal bank and looked down on fifty or sixty naked-headed vultures. At the sight of us, the birds spread their black wings and took off like huge vampires. The air reeked of decay.

The birds, we saw, were feeding not on Dajun but on thousands of dead fish.

James James didn't seem to mind the foul smell.

He stepped off the levee to the water's edge and walked along examining fish, plants, and weeds.

"Everything's dead or dying," he called, then reached into his back pocket and took out a jelly jar. He filled it with water from the canal and smelled it.

"Brackish," he said. "Salt water is killing the fresh-water life."

I slid down the embankment to his side.

"How does the salt get way up here?" I asked. "The bay is miles away."

"Some of it can come up the canal as the tides come and go, and some of it might come up through the soil." James James held up the jelly jar and studied it. "Fresh water," he said, "is lighter than salt water and floats on it—even in the ground. This is well country. If you pump off the fresh water for drinking and washing, the salt water rises and takes its place. Too many people are pulling off too much fresh water and letting the sea rise."

"We're not far from the condos," I said. "Is the salt getting into their wells?"

"Must be, and probably La Playa's municipal wells." The vultures stopped circling and dropped down on the dead fish again.

"Gumbo Limbo Hammock might be in trouble, too," he said. "We might have to move."

"Where would we go?" I cried, then considered a moment. "Mom and I'll be all right. She will soon buy a house, but where will Priscilla go—and Caruso? Where will he go?" I went on. "Not to mention you, the otter, the egrets, the anhingas, the bobcat, skunk, mink, and weasel—and Dajun. What can we do, James James?"

"We'll report this to the Director of the Water Management Department," he said. "I'll take this sample to him. He'll have to do something. In Miami they pump fresh water into the ground to push down the salt water. La Playa may have to do that, too. Expensive. Or we might have to dig wells farther inland, also expensive."

James James counted the dead fish in a small area and multiplied it by the size of the entire area to get an estimate of the number of fish killed. He made a note of each species. We were about to walk on down the canal toward the bay when he stopped.

"Liza K.," he said, "the salt intrusion from the bay can be stopped right here." He picked a twig from a tree and tasted it. "Buttonwood," he said. "For ages and ages buttonwood trees, which are very adaptable, have formed a barrier between the salt water and the fresh water. These ridges they make are natural dams.

"This is one of the canals that was built to drain the cypress swamp to build Silver City. The engineers dug the canal through the buttonwood ridge and left it open. Salt water comes in, and the fresh water drains out to sea. If the engineers put a dam here, the fresh water will seep back into the ground and push the salt water down below the well bottoms."

"Won't it back up and flood Silver City?" I asked.

"There are some lands on which nothing should be built in the first place," he said, "and a swamp is a primary one. Still, you're right—it will flood Silver City and we can't do that. I'll have a talk with the director."

We left the vultures to their feast. Their great wings swished like taffeta skirts as the birds rose, then dropped down and challenged each other for the fish. I looked back. Where the salt water was seeping upward into the land, the saw grass and cypress trees were dead or dying.

We walked home in silence.

"Get yourself dressed, Liza K.," James James said when we reached the hammock. "We need that map. I'll take Travis to that lake by the new houses."

"James James," I said when we reached the saw grass prairie, "would the salt water intrusion make blue-green algae grow?"

"No. Why do you ask?"

"I saw a mass of blue-green algae in Gumbo Limbo Hole when I was up in the oak tree."

"That's bad news," he said. "That means pollutants." He rubbed his forehead and frowned. "I didn't think Gumbo Limbo Hammock was on the watershed that drains the farms and septic tanks. Seems to me that the polluted runoff doesn't come our way. I'll have to check it again on the geology map."

"We sure need Dajun," I said. "Gumbo Limbo Hole is going to turn to scum. He really was our protecting dragon."

We came upon Caruso in his home in the mahogany grove. He was carving a fork from a piece of wood with his knife and talking to a friend called Beef Bones. Caruso often brought friends home for a bowl of Mom's soup.

"Where've you two been?" he asked.

"Looking for Dajun," I answered.

"H'aint found him yet?" He was smiling.

"No."

"Neither has the official." He winked, and his long bushy brows dipped over his deep-set black eyes. "I met him near the condo golf course this morning as I was going off to work. That man worries me to death. He's poking around here. Can't have him find me living out here like this; homeless, so to speak. He'll report me to the shelter and I'll have to live with nasty Mr. Burnster again." Caruso put down his whittling. "I just can't tolerate that Burnster. He's always telling me I can't sing worth a coyote. Just can't tolerate him, not even a minute."

"Then help us find Dajun, Caruso, so we can hide him." I pleaded. "Then the official will leave."

"Why would he do that?" the old singer asked.

"Eventually he'll think Dajun's dead and go away."

"What'll make him think that?"

"Without Dajun in the hole, in a very few days the blue-green algae and hydrilla will choke Gumbo Limbo Hole. Scum will cover it. That will tell the official that there is no alligator and he'll stop hunting him."

"That takes too long. I'll just tell him I saw a poacher shoot him," Caruso said smiling. "That'll make him quit hunting, *fortissimo*." He looked at his rumpled friend to see if he was impressing him.

"Good idea," Beef Bones said without moving his lips. Beef Bones was as thin as his name, and also smelly. I backed away, pulled James James's sleeve to come along, and started through the woods.

After leaving James James at the banyan tree, I went home by way of the solution pit to taste the water. It was fresh and sweet. It should have been salty. Things are mysterious in nature.

As I passed Priscilla's home, I saw that her card table was folded and hidden behind a tree. Her two bags of mini gin bottles were stuffed between the flanges of a cypress and she was nowhere in sight. I decided that she was afraid Travis would find her and had hidden somewhere. I didn't mean to pry, but as I looked around for her, I happened to see, tucked under the brown paper bags, many little packages of sugar like the kind you get for free in restaurants. Priscilla must stop in for coffee and collect them too. Nature is mysterious, but so are woods people.

5
Map Clues

James James gave me quite a surprise when I stepped out of the tent in my school clothes. He was dressed in chinos and a lightweight sports jacket.

"Wow!" I exclaimed.

"College leftovers," he said, and grinned. "Kind of dated, but they'll do."

I must have looked like the quintessential inquiring reporter, because he answered before I asked my question.

"I'm all dressed up because I'm going with you

to the County Government Center." I waited for what was going to follow that shocker.

"I want to tell the Director of the Water Management Department to plug that canal, Silver City or no Silver City. La Playa's drinking water is in jeopardy."

James James looked very handsome; he had even combed his hair and shaved. For all you could tell, he was any man going to work, and that made me think about James James and the war again. He never talked about Vietnam or what had affected him so deeply he could not work. Whatever it was, I knew it was painful. Sometimes when his face was at rest and he was watching Dajun or a bird, I could see the horror of war in his eyes. War must be even more hurtful than a father taking off his belt and whipping you.

We walked in silence to the Government Center. I was digesting the many surprises of the day: James James in business clothes, James James going to see the Director of the Water Management Department, and no Dajun in the culvert.

As we came out on the airport road, we ran into Caruso and Beef Bones. They were sitting on the ground beside a large plastic trash bag. I didn't recognize Caruso from a distance because he wasn't wearing his top hat. Upon coming closer, however, I saw the red feather stuck in the band of his cap.

"Caruso," I said. "What are you doing here?" He looked up and grinned.

"I'm working." He glanced at James James as if to apologize.

"What are you working at?" I asked, seeing that he was sitting at the curbside doing nothing.

"Beef Bones and I are waiting for my friend Sweeney. He has a toxic waste disposal plant. He needed some help picking up battery fluid and crankcase oil from garages." He gestured to the big bag. "Today he hired us to pick up and wash out these empty cans before he recycles them."

"What was in them?" James James asked.

"I don't know exactly," Caruso replied.

"It's wonderful you're helping," I said. I was glad to see an adult recycling. In La Playa it's mostly kids who do the work because one of our school assignments is to collect bottles, glass and plastic, tin cans, and newspapers. We separate them and put them in bins at school. Mom says there was a time when she and her folks never thought of recycling. They threw everything in the garbage and it was carted off to the dump and forgotten. Except it wouldn't be forgotten. The dumps became mountains, and the paint, spray cans, battery fluids, crankcase oil—the stuff Caruso was collecting—leaked into the soil. Presently the streams, rivers, lakes, and bays began to die. Poisoned fish made people sick. Now we recycle and kids do a lot of it.

"Where's Sweeney's plant, Caruso?" I asked. "I visited one last year with my class. I'll bet it's the same one."

"It's off Sable Palm Drive, near the canal," he answered.

"No," I said. "That's not the one."

"I didn't know you worked, Caruso," James James said, as if he were a little disappointed in Caruso for deserting him.

"Well, I must say," the singer offered by way of apology, "it hasn't been long. Beef Bones here got me into it. Said I should do something worthwhile. Liza K.'s Mom said recycling was worthwhile, so when Sweeney asked me to help, I said I would. I began work this morning and I'll be done as soon as Sweeney picks us up and we wash out these containers."

"That's a good thing to do, Caruso," I said.

"Well, why not," he replied. "As I said to Beef Bones, I'm only onstage for an hour or so each day, so why not help Sweeney and the nation. We're saving our pay to buy chickens for Dajun so he'll stay in the solution pit once you get him there, James James."

Caruso glanced at James James to see how he was taking this unusual news, but James James showed no reaction.

"Did you find Dajun?" Caruso finally asked.

"Not yet." James James was curt, and Caruso knew why.

"If you think I'm off my railroad track," he said, "you should check out your own engine. You look like the Duke of Windsor in that outfit, James James."

"We're off to the County Government Center," James James said. "We need a map to find Dajun."

"The County Government Center?" Caruso's eyes narrowed. "Now don't you go telling them social workers I'm living in the woods. They'll put me in that shelter with Mr. Burnster."

"I'm not going near the social workers, Caruso," James James said, "and even if I ran into one and he knocked me down and banged my head on the cement to find out, I wouldn't tell him where you lived. Never."

The noon sun was sparkling on the long slender needles of the slash pines when we reached the Government Center. We hesitated; then James pointed to a roster of departments and room numbers on an outdoor plaque. The Water Management Department and the Natural Resources Department were both in building D. We found it and parted company at the door.

After being sent from one person to another, I finally met a woman who knew what I wanted. Her name was Clara Lee Dade and she was very pleased that I was interested in the county's natural resources. She opened a drawer and took out the map I had seen with my sixth-grade class. Carefully she spread it flat on her desk. The details were even more useful than I remembered.

"All the land elevations are here," I said excitedly. "Look, here's the prairie, the pines, and Gumbo Limbo Hammock." I ran my finger over the familiar landscape and hunched closer to the map.

"I didn't know there was hammock there," Ms. Dade said, looking more closely. "Are you sure there's a hammock on that piece of land?"

I thought of James James's promise to Caruso and told her I must be mistaken, but she would not be thrown off. She leaned more closely over the map.

"Could be you're right," she said. "The elevation checks out. There's high land there." She opened a file, took out a paper, and came back.

"Could be you're right, all right. That whole section in there lies between the highway, the airport road, and the condos. It belongs to the old Cypress Railroad Company. The railroad failed long ago and the land has been quite forgotten." I was glad to hear we weren't living on county property where we could be evicted.

"If a hammock is there," she went on, "it's a rare find. There are not many left in Collier County." She straightened up and looked at me. "Hammocks are tropical Edens."

I was very sorry I had mentioned the hammock.

Picking up the map, I hurried toward the door.

"I might come over and take a look at it," she said, and I spun around and faced her.

"I don't think you'd like it," I said, making a yukky face. "It's a mess. It's in a jungle of tourists, carbon dioxide from traffic, and condos."

"Guess so," she said sadly. "We cement over or drain everything in this country. You should have seen Collier County when I grew up." Her face softened as she called up her memories. "Do you think it's worth my while to check it out?" she persisted.

"No, I really don't," I said firmly. "It will make you sad. Tin cans, blue-green algae—no alligators, dead snapping turtles . . ."

"Yes," she said and to my relief turned her attention to her job. She opened a cash drawer, "That will be five dollars."

"Five dollars?" My heart sank. I had no money and I needed that map right now. Travis was hunting Dajun.

"Oh," I said, collecting my thoughts. "When I was here with my class from Royal Palm School, the man in charge said these maps were free."

"Are you in Miss Wilson's sixth-grade class, the

class that is studying the ecology of southern Florida?"

"Yes, I am," I said. "We're supposed to do some research over the holidays. I wanted this map, but I don't have any money to pay for it."

"That's all right." She went to a drawer and took out a pad.

"Your name and address is all I'll need if you're in Miss Wilson's class." I hesitated. Now what should I do?

"Liza K.," I began, pausing before I gave my last name.

"Do you spell that K-a-y or C-a-y?"

"K-a-y as in Katherine with a K," I answered.

She wrote down Kay for my last name.

"Your address?"

I saw the faces of James James, Priscilla, Caruso, and even his friend Beef Bones. I saw Travis rounding the hole looking for Dajun, his finger on the trigger of his gun.

"It's 1345 Ninth Avenue," I whispered, and I hoped she would never check. I had given her the address of the diner.

"That's all," she said smiling. "It's yours—free."

"Thank you so much."

I forced myself to walk, not run, out of the room and down the corridor. I passed the office of the Director of the Water Management Department, saw James James leaning over a stack of papers consulting with a burly person, and went right on and out the front door into the sunshine.

I did not wait for James James. He had looked as if he was involved in something that would take a long time. I had to get back and find Dajun. Travis would not be fooled much longer by lakes on a golf course. I ran home.

When I was back in my woods-people outfit— blue jeans, ragged T-shirt, and sneakers—I spread the map on our table under the cool oak and, with a peanut butter sandwich for lunch, sat down to study it carefully.

Good. There were at least three places Dajun could be: that slough that seeped into the cypress swamp; a hole the county had dug for road material—borrow pits, they are called; and a little nature park by the condos with trails, benches, and grass. In the center was an artificial lake. No underground caves were marked on the map.

Before starting out, I climbed the oak to see if Dajun had by any chance come back to Gumbo

Limbo Hole. The water was crystal clear, the frogs were swimming, the birds were stalking the fish, and the otter was sleeping at the mouth of his den. The light was behind me, and again I could see to the bottom of the hole. No Dajun.

Then I glanced at the canal James James had checked this morning. It looked more like a vegetable garden than a waterway. Gumbo Limbo Hole was the only clean water in the whole area.

But even it was threatened. That large evil patch of blue-green algae was still in the pit and growing. I almost cried. The pollutants were reaching our Eden after all.

"Dajun! Come back—we need you," I said right out loud. "Come back before our sparkling hole is scum like the rest of La Playa's waterways."

Back on the ground I took the armadillos' trail across the pineland to the cypress swamp. I often went to the edge of this swamp chasing butterflies, but had never gone in—it was very mucky. Now I must. After a few steps I found I could walk on the hummocks of tough grass and on the enormous stumps of the felled cypress trees. Before very long I was quite taken up with this world. I found an empty woodpecker nest, saw a fish hawk high in a tree, and watched a huge snake grab a cotton rat. An opossum clung to a limb with a baby clinging to her back. They stared at me and I blew them a kiss. Butterflies hovered over tree flowers.

The slough in the swamp was easy to find now that I had seen it on the map. As I came upon it, I saw the dorsal spikes of an alligator jutting above the water. I splashed toward the animal and stopped. The spikes did not belong to Dajun. They were much too small.

"Hello, pretty girl." I jumped, lost my balance, and grabbed a vine to right myself.

"Hello, pretty girl." The masculine voice sounded like Travis's, but not quite. I didn't answer.

"Are you all right, mother?"

Mother? I breathed easier. The person wasn't talking to me. Then I realized that this was far worse. There were people in the swamp. The reward, I thought. The people from the condos know about the reward and are searching for Dajun.

"Hello, hello." The voice seemed to be coming from the far side of a strangler fig. I hid behind a huge cypress and peered out.

"You look a lot better."

Look a lot better? Was someone sick? I decided right then and there to leave. I stole quietly out of the swamp and ran through the pine woods back to Gumbo Limbo Hammock, satisfied that Dajun was not in the cypress slough. The water was not deep enough. His back would have projected six inches out of the water even if he had been lying on the bottom. Dajun was two and a half feet thick from his belly to the tip of the rugged scutes on his back.

Priscilla had put up her table again and was writing when I came into the gumbo limbo grove.

"Where have you been, Priscilla?" I asked. "I thought you had left us."

"I've been sitting by the little lake in the nature center at the condos watching that Travis man. He's been asking everyone if they've seen Dajun."

"Did he find him?"

"No, he didn't." I was glad to hear that. I would not have to check the condo lake. She smiled. I smiled.

"He offered anyone a reward who could find

him, then went home," Priscilla went on. "I watched him drive off toward Silver City about an hour ago."

I was right, the person I'd heard in the swamp a few minutes ago hadn't been Travis. That was bad news in one way. With so many eyes, and now so many people aware of the reward, someone was bound to find him and perhaps even shoot him.

Priscilla had not only put up her card table and palm roof again but returned her mini bottle bag and sugar packets to the side of her wicker loveseat. The woods looked like home once more, and I felt courageous enough to ask her what the bottles and sugar were for. I opened my mouth to speak.

"Is it hard to write about Dajun when he's not around to inspire you?" I heard myself say instead of what I had in my mind.

"No," she answered. "My poetry has new poignancy—the empty hole, the deserted beach, the lonely call of the dove, and silent step of the turtle." She bent over her pad and did not look up.

"Mom brought home shrimp bisque this morning," I said, smacking my lips. "Yummm."

"That's very nice, Liza K.," she said, "but I'm not hungry at all."

"I know," I replied. "I'll just leave it on this stump. You can give it to the raccoons so Mom's feelings won't be hurt."

"That's a lovely idea," she said, and bit the end of her pencil as she looked off into space like a real poet.

6

Complications

Returning home along the armadillo trail, I thought I found a clue to the mystery of our missing dragon. The armadillos, those fancy mammals who look like Sir Galahad in their plates of horny armor, had made a path that came right up to the hammock, then turned abruptly and looped back into the pines. Something in Gumbo Limbo Hammock was driving them off. Since armadillos eat underground insects and insect larvae by digging them out of the earth with long claws and snouts, I concluded it was the saltwater deposit they were avoiding. It must have risen up into the soil and killed the insects. If that had happened, it must also have reached the Hole and driven Dajun away.

I did not think about it long, however. As I came home around the live oak tree, I saw Mom stirring the shrimp bisque. Her shoulders were slumped instead of straight up and her head was bowed low. I bolted to her.

"What's the matter?" I asked, fearing my father had found us.

"I don't think I'll get the job," she said, and I breathed again.

"Why?" I asked.

"A young man from business school was interviewed today. He'll get it. They always give managerial jobs to the men."

"Not always," I said. "Besides, you can do a better job than anyone." I meant that. Mom does everything well when she has time, including fishing and pitching tents.

"Liza K., Liza K.," she said pacing before the stove, "I've got to have that job. I must get you out of here and into a proper home."

"This is a proper home," I said. "I love it here. I

want to stay in Gumbo Limbo Hammock forever."

She shook her head and clucked her tongue as she stirred the pot.

"One important thing did happen today," she said brightly. "The social worker called to tell me your father has gone north to a clinic for therapy." I studied her to see if that was good or bad news. Her face was serene.

Then a happy thought struck her. She spun on her toes and took my hands.

"You and I can start a new life," she said. "Home or homeless, fancy job or no fancy job, we have each other without having to worry about your father anymore." She hugged me and, pressing my head to her shoulder, rocked gently. The pain of those long-ago punishments flowed down my spine and out my toes.

"I hope he finds a nice place to live," I said, and I meant it. He was my father.

James James did not get back to Gumbo Limbo Hammock until Mom and I were finishing our shrimp bisque. His appearance was announced by a gasp from Mom.

"Is something wrong?" James James asked.

"You're so dressed up," she said. He laughed, then turned to me.

"Did you find Dajun?"

"No," I said. "But I have my suspicions—salt in our soil and the hole drove him off." I hesitated. It didn't sound quite reasonable. I thought about it again—but could not come up with a better reason.

"There's no salt in Gumbo Limbo Hammock, yet," James James assured me.

I agreed: Certainly it was not in the solution hole. It was fresh as dawn.

"Any luck with the map?" he asked.

"Yes," I said. "I didn't find any underground caves, but I did find three good hiding spots. Dajun was not in number one. Priscilla unknowingly checked number two and he's not there— I'm on my way to number three. What about you? Will the director of the Water Department plug up the canal, James James?"

"Let me begin at the beginning," James James said. "First of all, the director was shocked to hear about the saltwater intrusion and the dead fish. Water is a big issue in this town—the environmentalists are fighting the developers, the

developers are trying to get around the environmentalists, and the politicians are hopping from
one to another."

"But fish are dying," I said incredulously. "That
means bad water for people." I couldn't imagine a
director not doing what was good for his community.

"The situation is serious," James James said.
"Salt is getting into the condo wells—and—the
town wells."

"It is?" Mom asked. "That's a worry. Many people in La Playa are elderly and on salt-free diets.
What can be done?"

"James James wants to close the canals," I told
her. "The fresh water will back up, sink into the
ground where it ought to be, and push down the
salt water."

"I'm afraid it's not that simple," James James
said. "Florida's vast network of waterways affects
many special interests, like housing, farming,
tourism, and wildlife."

"We get a lot of elderly people in the diner,"
Mom said, pursuing the salt matter. "I guess we
should use bottled water."

"You should," James James said. "The town

water's safe now for most people, but not for many of the elderly."

"Hmmm," said Mom, and handed James James a cup of shrimp bisque.

He gulped a mouthful and smacked his lips.

"I don't understand why it's not simple," Mom said. "Plug the canals and move the people. Water is life."

James James put down his cup and opened a satellite map of southern Florida.

"I'll show you why," he said, and waved his hand across the map. "The view is from Lake Okeechobee to the Florida Bay. Before you lie 14,000 miles of levees and canals. Here we are." He pointed to La Playa and took another swallow of soup, then spread the map on the ground. "Look how Mother Nature's plan for the Everglades has been tortured and diverted." He swirled his fingers over the maze of canals.

"Here's how it happened. The Everglades, which is really a slow river, is so rich with soil and nutrients that the Army Corps of Engineers was engaged to drain it for farmland below Lake Okeechobee." The map plainly showed that where once swampy river had flowed there were now houses, towns, and farms. They covered many square miles.

"To drain the river," James James went on, "the engineers built these canals going east to the ocean"—he pointed—"and these going south. They built locks and dams, protected some areas as water conservation areas, and eventually exposed this rich black river bottom. Sugarcane and other crops were planted. As time went on, the crops were fertilized and sprayed. Nutrients and chemicals came down the Everglades River, around the hammocks, into the saw grass and sloughs; and the river changed. Weeds grew in the nutrients and choked out the fish. Birds died for lack of fish and the mammals disappeared. The Everglades National Park protects what wildlife remains, but it is losing the battle. I keep this map to remind myself why humans can't improve on a swamp. You change one thing and you change the whole ecosystem."

"So why don't we just block up the canals and hold the water where it ought to be?" Mom persisted from her hands and knees.

"Maybe we will." James James said. "One governor promised to close the canals and restore the natural flow of the Everglades, but he never got the money from the legislators. Maybe the next one will. We can still bring back the Everglades and restore good drinking water."

Mom was still interested in the salt and asked again what could be done about that.

"The director said La Playa will have to drill wells farther inland. And if that doesn't work, the town may have to install a desalinator, one of those plants that take salt out of sea water. They are very expensive. For the time being people will have to stop watering lawns and filling swimming pools." I listened, but all this water talk was not finding Dajun, although I did think it would make a good report for Miss Wilson. Right now time was running out for the dragon.

And it was running out for the woods people, too. Many outsiders were learning about Gumbo Limbo Hammock. There was Ms. Clara Lee Dade, the Director of the Water Management Department, and those people from the condos I had heard in the swamp. Very soon someone was going to find our alligator. A hundred dollars was a hundred dollars. And very soon they would walk into the hammock and find us.

"James, James," I said interrupting the water talk, "if salt hasn't run Dajun out of here, and he has food, and it's not the mating season, then where is he?"

James James took a breath and looked at his notes. "Something else might have happened to him. There was a large amount of pentachlorophenol—PCP—in that water sample," he said. "PCP is a toxic chemical used as an herbicide to kill weeds and fungus. We use a lot of it in Florida. It is primarily a wood preservative. PCP is used heavily in this warm, moist climate to preserve houses, boardwalks, telephone posts—all kinds of wood products—and it's getting into the canal—from where I don't know, probably from everywhere."

"If it's coming from everywhere," said Mom, getting to her feet, "why aren't fish dying in all the canals? Why just that one spot?"

James James shook his head and refolded the map.

"How do you know it was PCP?" Mom asked with sudden curiosity.

"Years ago I used to analyze the drinking water for a citizen's group in my hometown. Collier

County has a lab, so I asked the director if I could go there and test my sample for pollutants other than salt. I found it loaded with PCP. Enough to make people sick, retard growth, cause lesions, and impair reproduction in other mammals and birds."

"That's awful," I said. "What's the director going to do about *that?*"

"At first he pooh-poohed me about its effects. Then I showed him a U.S. Fish and Wildlife Service report in his own library detailing the hazards of PCP to fish, wildlife, and invertebrates." He glanced at Mom. "Those are snails, insects, crabs."

"I know," she said, and then laughed. "With a daughter like mine, I can't avoid knowing things like that." James James smiled at me and went on.

"The director was shocked. Then he remembered the county had been using PCP in heavy doses to kill the weeds around the borrow pit to make way for picnic tables and benches. The pit is about a hundred yards from where we found the dead fish, Liza K. That hard rain a week ago could have carried the PCP into the canal in one flush—except . . . I can't quite see how the runoff got past that levee we climbed, Liza K.—but it must have."

"The borrow pit?" I said. "Could the chemical have washed into the borrow pit?"

"Easily," he answered. "Why?"

"Dajun might be hiding there."

"Slim chance," said James James.

Mom got to her feet. "Wherever he is, he better be safe. We just have to have Dajun around until we all have good homes and"—she looked at James James—"good jobs."

"James James," I interrupted. "Dajun really could be in the borrow pit." I unfolded my map. "He could get there by going down this wet valley beyond the saw grass prairie and into this old irrigation ditch in that abandoned tomato field." I pointed. "From the ditch to the pit is about forty feet. He could have crossed without anyone seeing him. He's like lightning when he wants to be." James James rubbed his shaven chin. He did not seem to be hearing me.

"Want to come to the pit with me?" I asked, tapping him on the arm.

"No, you go ahead, Liza K.," he said. "I told the director I would ask the manager of the golf course if he was using PCP as a fungicide."

"Hmmm," I said, and washed my soup cup in the bucket of soap suds Mom keeps for the dishes. I had learned in environmental studies class that soap doesn't harm streams and waterways, so we woods people use soap, not detergents. Detergents have phosphates in them. The use of phosphates has been reduced since it was discovered that they took the oxygen out of the water and killed just about every living thing in the lakes and streams. I checked the detergents in the supermarket to see if the companies really had gotten rid of the phosphates. It's almost true. Some laundry detergents have less than 0.5 percent, but some still have 5 and 6 percent. Dishwasher detergents have 8.1 percent, so Mom and I decided soap was best for our hammock. Soap is made of fat or oil, alkali, and salt, which don't harm the plants and animals and you—and the dishes get just as clean.

Mom poured a cup of soup for Priscilla, got her towel, soap, and bathing cap, and headed for the lake for a swim-bath before sleeping and going to work at eleven P.M.

"Take the soup to Priscilla on your way to the

borrow pit, Liza K.," Mom called. I turned to James James.

"Are you sure you don't want to come with me?"

"I'll meet you there when I'm done," he answered. I could tell he didn't think Dajun was in the borrow pit, but I had to be sure.

Picking up my map and Priscilla's soup, I started off. It had been a long day, and it still was not done.

Priscilla was not in her gumbo limbo tree camp, so I left the soup on her table. As I turned to go, I saw that her notebook was open. I shouldn't have, but I turned a page to read a poem. There was none. I flipped on. All the pages were blank. I couldn't believe it. Priscilla was always leaning over that book writing poems. Maybe it wasn't this book—yes it was. She had plastered a design on the cover with the sticky leaves of a funny plant called the poor-man's-patch. I've mended holes in my shirt with them. They don't wash off.

The blank pages scared me. Then I recalled that some poets work on their poems in their heads for years before writing them down. That's what Priscilla does, I said to myself, and walked quickly away.

The borrow pit is on cleared pineland. James James says he gathers coontie there, a starchy delicious plant the Seminole Indians used to eat like we eat potatoes. As I walked toward it, I thought about Priscilla. Maybe the kids at school were right about her—she was crazy. No, I argued, Priscilla is intelligent and kind. She, like the hammock, is frayed and battered on the outside, but full of good things on the inside. Then I remembered her mini bottles.

In this preoccupied state of mind I found myself standing in the abandoned tomato field. It was now covered with weeds. Instead of walking among pines, wild grasses, and sable palms, I was knee deep in ragweed, morning glory vines, and a pest called Brazilian holly from South America.

I stopped still.

Priscilla was bent over like a potato digger in the middle of the field.

"Priscilla," I called running toward her. "Your soup's getting cold."

I paused a few steps from her. She was tying a mini gin bottle full of red liquid on a bush. The little bottle shone brightly when the sun struck it.

"Getting ready for the Christmas holidays?" I asked for lack of anything better to say.

"Come here, Liza K.," she said, sinking to the ground, her dusty brown skirt billowing around her. "Sit down. In a moment, you'll see something incredibly beautiful." I sat.

A soft whir sounded at my ear and I felt a cool breeze.

"He thinks you're a flower," Priscilla whispered.

"Who?" I asked, trying to see my ear. A red metallic light flashed, then a purple-green one. A hummingbird flew over my shoulder, hesitated by my yellow earring, and flew on. It hovered at the mouth of the mini gin bottle, dipped in its long slender beak, and drank.

"Priscilla," I gasped. "You feed the hummingbirds."

"What did you think I did with the minis and sugar packets?" She frowned at me as if I were accusing her of some evil.

"Well," I stammered, "I just didn't know."

"Look." She pointed. Five more little hummingbirds hovered over bottles tied to dried weeds and saw palmettos. Trembling with excitement, Priscilla clasped her hands under her chin.

"Aren't they exquisite?"

"They are," I whispered as tiny bodies refracted red, purple, green, and gold lights and the sound of little wings filled the air.

At last I knew what Priscilla did with the mini gin bottles, and it was wonderful—it was truly a beautiful thing. I wished the kids at school could see this.

The whir and darting of small wings had distracted me for too long. I jumped to my feet.

"Priscilla," I said, helping her up, "come with me. I think Dajun is in the borrow pit. And he may be very sick."

7

The Red Feather

The borrow pit water was soupy with blue-green algae and hopeless to see through. Priscilla and I walked around it. We were looking for claw or tail marks Dajun might have made coming in and out of the water.

"No sensible alligator would come near this foul place," Priscilla finally said. "The water looks absolutely poisonous and all the plants around it are dead."

"The county's killing them to make a picnic park," I said. "But it's killing lots more than weeds." I told her about the fish in the canal.

"You say the vultures ate the fish?"

"Yes."

"Will they die from eating the PCP-killed fish?"

"I don't know," I said, horrified to think that it might kill not only the vultures but gulls, raccoons, crabs, little alligators—everything that eats dead fish. I had wondered minutes ago if Priscilla was crazy. Well, I had my answer. She wasn't.

"I really don't think he's here," she said. "So let's get back to Gumbo Limbo Hole and scare that old dragon away before Travis returns to look for him after his supper. He told a lady in the nature park he was coming back."

"He did?"

"He's hunting him hard," Priscilla said.

"Well, that's good," I said. "Dajun knows a hunter when he sees one, and he hides."

"You think he's hiding?" she asked.

"I do, but I don't know where."

"Under this slime," she said. "Maybe he's here after all."

"Maybe," I answered. "How long can an alligator hold its breath?"

"If the water is cold, five hours, I read some-where," she answered.

"But the water is still very warm. It's only De-cember."

"Then he's hiding where there is water *and* air."

"Where's that?"

"Right here in the borrow pit. When the water is low you can see a cavern on the side of the pit."

"A cavern?"

"Yes, I saw it last spring at the height of the dry season before the rains came and covered it. It goes far back and slants upward. The opening is underwater now, but the ceiling inside is high. There would be air in it."

Priscilla walked to a large chunk of limestone rock that had been dumped on the shore by the pit digger.

"It's right down from this. About two feet."

I picked up a stick and after swishing the algae away reached back. There was a cavern.

"Let's gather Brazilian holly leaves," I said.

"For a trap?" she asked.

"Of a sort," I replied. "We'll scatter the leaves on top of the algae, and if Dajun comes out of the cave to eat, he'll make a track through the leaves.

We'll know he's here."

"That sounds like a good plan," Priscilla said.

It was almost dark when we got home. Mom was asleep; the woods were quiet. I asked Priscilla if she would like some tea and lit the Coleman stove. Presently James James arrived.

"Sorry I didn't meet you," he said. "Any luck?"

"No, but maybe." I told him about the cavern. "How about you?"

"The golf course does not use PCP. And I just checked the picnic area on the way home. The PCP could not have washed into the canal. As I suspected, the levee's too high."

We sipped tea listening to the insects and an incredible mockingbird who was singing to the rising moon.

"There's a magnolia warbler in these woods," James James said.

"How do you know?" Priscilla asked excitedly.

"The mockingbird is imitating it," he said. "A magnolia warbler is rare." He leaned back and looked up at the night forest. "Gumbo Limbo Hammock is one of the last islands for some of our most beautiful birds."

"And several butterflies," I said.

"There are two hummingbirds here that have never been recorded in Florida," Priscilla said. Then, looking around to be sure no one but we two were listening, she whispered, "And a rare lignum vitae tree, worth thousands and thousands of dollars." We lapsed into silence again.

The owls began their courtship calls and the raccoons came down from the trees to hunt for crayfish along the shore of Gumbo Limbo Hole.

"I was offered a job today," James James said, breaking the spell.

"You were?" I said. "By the director?"

"Yeah."

"Did you take it?"

"No."

"Good," said Priscilla, and got to her feet. "Too many people working now. Good night, dear friends. I left my poetry out on the table. Those mischievous little raccoons will be tearing the pages if I don't get back. Thank you for the tea."

"And for the cold soup?" I teased. "You'd better bring it back and I'll heat it up."

"No, thank you," she said politely. "I don't really want it." She hesitated in the darkness. "Where did you say you put it?"

Priscilla rustled off in the moonlight, her dress touching the leaves of a bush that sent an explosion of sweet perfume into the air.

"James James," I said when she was gone, "I know what Priscilla does with her mini gin bottles."

"She has a purpose for them?" He seemed surprised.

"She fills them with red sugar water and hangs them out for the hummingbirds."

James James whistled very softly. "I sure had her figured wrong," he said.

"And she doesn't write poems to Dajun. At least she doesn't put them down on paper."

He whistled again. "As I said, I sure had her figured wrong." I didn't ask him what he had figured. It didn't matter now. If I had learned nothing else from nature, I had learned that once the butterfly steps into the light, it can't go back into the cocoon.

We looked out through the trees and thought our thoughts.

"James James," I finally said. "Why didn't you take the job? You are really needed."

"I like helping out," he answered. "But I can do

a lot more for us by hanging loose. You take a job and someone above you tells you what to do. Your own ideas are squelched."

"I see." I said, but I didn't quite.

James James got up and washed his teacup. "I haven't seen Caruso since we met him on the road," he said. "Have you?"

"No, but he told me he had a big concert tonight at the old railroad station. He must be there right now."

James James patted my head as if I were a child and I resented it. What was he saying to me with that condescending pat? He stretched his long arms.

"I've got to get up early, Liza K.," he said. "The director wants me to look at the canal with him and his engineer. See if we can close it."

A soft rain fell soon after I crawled into my sleeping bag. I lay awake listening to the water drop through the oak leaves sounding like the feet of those little tree lizards. Mom arose, dressed by candlelight, and leaned over me for a moment. Then she kissed me good night.

When her footsteps died away, I thought about the job she wanted so badly and the young man who might get it. I thought about Priscilla and James James not wanting a job, and then and there gave up trying to figure out people. I drifted off to sleep.

Early in the morning I awoke. I started thinking about the hammock. Rare birds and butterflies were here. The water of the solution pit was pure enough to drink. Gumbo Limbo Hammock was a rare and beautiful phenomenon and Dajun was a big reason why it was. I would tell Travis that. He must not shoot him for that reason alone.

Say that again, Liza K., I said sitting up, and I did. "Dajun," I said out loud, "is the reason why Gumbo Limbo Hammock is beautiful."

So he had to be there. He hadn't died or left. He was right in Gumbo Limbo Hole. It was so obvious. The water was clear—all but a few spots of blue-green algae. The invertebrates were healthy, the fish, reptiles, birds and mammals were happy—except for the armadillos—but they're in the pinelands. I see it. I see it, I said to myself. The clear, beautiful environment was saying— Dajun is in Gumbo Limbo Hole.

I couldn't go back to sleep. In great excitement

I got up and dressed, although it was only six thirty. The great horned owl flew out of the oak when I moved the orange crate under it. Waving to him, I climbed to the top.

The sun came up.

The water turned silver and blue. The reeds came into view. Finally I saw the beach.

"He's not there," I cried. And I had been so sure of it.

"Where are you?" I snapped. "I know you're there."

The light brightened and I saw that both patches of blue-green algae were gone, the one under the royal palm and the one on the side of the deep hole. Dajun must have bulldozed them up on the land. I would find them and at least show everyone the evidence that proved he was there.

Scrambling down the tree, I circled the lake, concentrating on finding the algae. Suddenly Travis appeared on Gumbo Limbo Trail. He was walking straight toward me. Taking a complete about-face turn, I tiptoed to the armadillo trail in the pineland and sat down behind a palmetto.

I heard a soft grunt and an armadillo pattered

out of the bushes and rolled—they don't seem to walk—right past me. He stopped to dig into a fire ant nest. The ants crawled over his armor but could not penetrate it. Those that found his bare ears were easily displaced with a claw. I moved and he saw me. Sedately he eyed me and rolled on into the pinelands. He could have hidden in the dense foliage of Gumbo Limbo Hammock, but he didn't. And then I knew why.

A hammock is not part of your "niche," I said to the odd fellow. You came from the southwest, where your ancestors fed on scorpions, fire ants, roaches, and tarantulas—in the pines and cha-parral—never in a rich, moist hammock. It's just not your dish of oatmeal. That's why your trail ends at the hammock, and not because the soil is tainted with salt.

I was pleased. If you hang around the woods long enough, you will figure out all the answers. The next answer I wanted was the one-hundred-dollar one—where was Dajun? The answer was there, but not quite there.

"I'm close, close, close," I said. "But not quite close enough. I've got to figure out what's going on before Travis does. He must be close to solving the mystery too."

I ran back to my tent, picked up my rod, and met him on Dajun's beach.

"Hello," I said.

"You again?" he said. "I didn't expect to see you out here."

"But the 'gator's gone," I said.

"Where did you hear that?"

"I'm not sure," I answered. "Oh, yes, someone said you got him."

"Well, I didn't, but somebody must have. He's hasn't surfaced for a week."

I cast my line. It plunked far out near the pit in the hole.

Reeling in slowly, I watched the blinking water wondering if Dajun was in that deep hole. It's cold down there. He wouldn't have to breathe very often.

That was impossible. I had just looked into it from the tree and he wasn't there.

"Did you hear about all the fish that were killed in the canal near the county borrow pit?" I asked Travis.

"No," he said. "But the Director of the Water Management Department left word for me to call him. I'll bet that's what it's about. He hires me to clean up messes like that. I'll check it out. Where did you say the dead fish were?"

I told him, then added, "After you get beyond the prairie, just follow the turkey vultures."

He picked up his binoculars and scanned the hole and then the saw grass prairie once more.

"Beats me," he said. "I've been hunting for this guy for ten days and I haven't seen a keel or an eye bone. A poacher must have beat me to it." He fingered the gun in his holster. "Thanks for telling me about the fish," he said, and walked off between the willows. I stood stone still until I was sure he was far away. Then I relaxed.

Ten days, I said. Hmmm. More proof Dajun's right here. Ten days is long enough for the hydrilla to grow masses; and there isn't any, and long enough for that clump of blue-green algae to spread; and it hasn't.

"Hello."

I started.

"Mother, are you all right?" I froze. That same voice.

"Gugh ugh ugh ughaaaaa rrrrrrrrrr."

"James James," I said as I recognized his call to

Dajun. He had found our good dragon and was calling him. I put down my rod and pushed through the willows to greet him. He wasn't there.

"Hello, pretty girl."

I looked up. On a tree limb sat a gray parrot.

"Well," I gasped in astonishment. "Where did you come from?"

"Qimmiq, do you want to go out?"

"Hey, you're pretty wonderful," I said. "Someone must miss you very much." I picked up a stick and held it in front of his feet. He stepped on it and I brought him down to my face.

"Hello, yourself," I said.

The parrot cocked his head and pinned a black pupil in a yellow iris on me. The pupil expanded and contracted.

"You're a beautiful bird," he said, the white feathers around his eyes gleaming.

"I am?" I answered. "That's nice. I'm happy to meet you. Real, real happy. The woods are not full of people after all." I stroked the bird's beak, and he lifted his feathers to say he liked me.

"Thank you," I said. He stretched up his wings. His tail was carmine red.

"Caruso's hat," I said. "It was you who decorated Caruso's hat. At last I know where that feather came from."

Sidling along the stick to my arm, he walked up to my shoulder. He seemed content, so I carried him around the hole looking for blue green algae. There was none we could see, but there was a mound of bladderworts, a water plant, piled up by the alligator flags.

"He *is* here," I caroled. "He *is* here. But he also isn't here.

"Where is he?" I said to the parrot, then put up my hand and he stepped on it. I brought him in front of my face and looked at him hard. "You know where he is, don't you?" I said. "Where is he?"

"You're a beautiful bird. Night, night."

"You're a very frustrating parrot," I answered. "You talk, but you don't talk."

I walked back to my tent with the bird on my shoulder. I was not going to put him back in the willows where I had found him. He was telling me something, something important that I hadn't yet thought about. Opening my bird book, I discovered he was an African gray parrot. "The best talker of all the parrots," the book said.

I certainly agreed with that. This bird could imitate not only people but an alligator—or James James calling an alligator. Maybe that was it. He had heard James James calling Dajun. The old dragon hadn't roared since the last breeding season.

The friendly parrot let me rub my nose against his beak, then nipped me gently on the ear.

"Gugh ugh ugh ugh, night, night," he roared.

"Gugh—night?" I repeated. "Sir bird," I hooted, "you've just solved the mystery of the missing alligator. I am going to name you Sherlock Holmes."

8

The Word of Sherlock Holmes

Now that Sherlock Holmes had told me where Dajun was hiding, I had to wait all day to find him. Waiting is always difficult, but this wait was a torment. Travis had returned and was hiding in the willows at the back of the beach, which I took to mean he also had solved the mystery of the missing Dajun.

To allay my nervousness and pass the time, I fixed a big breakfast and ate it when Mom came home. Later, to kill more time, I looked for butterfly caterpillars to raise. I found one I didn't know, a prickly red-spined thing with yellow and black stripes. I picked the leaf it was feeding on and some others like it and put them in my bug cage. In a week or so it would become a pupa, and some weeks or months later an otherworldly butterfly. As it dried its wings in the air, I would look it up in my butterfly book, check it off on my checklist, and let it go. If I am lucky, I find butterfly eggs and watch from act one to act four. When I lived in town, I used to pretend I was an egg, a caterpillar, a chrysallis—and finally a butterfly. I would fly up in the air and soar out over the trees on my shimmering wings to unknown flowers and gardens. I haven't played that game since I came to the woods.

I also found a tiny orchid that my book says is rare. Every time I poked among the trees and vines, I would find another amazing survivor in Gumbo Limbo Hammock. James James calls this spot "our planet's last holdout against the invasion of people."

I still had hours to go, so I joined Priscilla. She was refilling her minis with red sugar water. I held them while she poured. I also helped her hang them. While out in the pineland she suggested we look at the Brazilian holly leaves. I wasn't ready to tell Priscilla where Dajun was hiding, so I went to the borrow pit with her. The leaves, of course, floated undisturbed on the scum.

Busy as I tried to make myself, time, nevertheless, moved like a Florida gopher turtle. The day would not end, and Travis was putting two and two together.

I left Priscilla mixing red vegetable dye in sugar water and went back to the hole to keep an eye on Travis. I wondered why he never came into the hammock. I was certainly glad he didn't, but it did seem odd that he had never put his foot in this beautiful place. Then I remembered he was an alligator hunter. Alligator hunters stay where alligators are—in the wetlands—and don't waste time in dry lands. Just as a hammock is not an armadillo's niche, so it is not an alligator's or an alligator hunter's. Travis stayed in the dragon's niche, and as long as he did, we woods people were safe.

For the next hour I read a book by the hole, then climbed the oak the better to spy on the hunter. He was walking toward the saw grass prairie. I squealed joyously into my fists. If he was going there at this hour he did *not* know where the old dragon was after all.

At a clump of cabbage palms he sat down, and I smirked no more. He was watching the beach. He did know. And he had his gun out. I almost cried.

Mom came home from her school. She looked for me in the tent, then up in the tree. I could see her face far down below between limbs and leaves. It was radiant. Something wonderful had happened. I had one hour to go. As swiftly as a lizard I dropped from limb to limb and landed on the ground before her.

"You got the job," I said.

"Yes, I did! I start tomorrow. No more night work." She lifted her head proudly. "And it's even better than that. I'm manager of not one but two diners. The boss is opening another at the north end of town."

"Two," I said in admiration. "You are manager of two diners? Wow, Mom, you really *are* good. See, I told you so."

"The house," she said without waiting for any more compliments. "I can buy the white house. The papers are not ready but I want to leave here said. "I think they're busy." I looked at the alarm clock. It was six thirty. One half hour to go. I left Mom packing her clothes and crept to the water's edge to watch Travis. If he was going to shoot Dajun, I would scream bloody murder and make him miss.

To my surprise Travis put his binoculars in their case and turned toward the trail. I couldn't believe it. Was he actually leaving? I closed my eyes and opened them. He had disappeared into the jungle. Absentmindedly I picked a flower and chewed its stem. I breathed shallow breaths. Then I heard Travis's car engine start, turn over, and move off, growing fainter and fainter. He was gone. I ran back to the tent.

"Mom," I said, my heart thumping a farewell fanfare to the alligator hunter, "Travis doesn't know where Dajun is. I thought he did. I thought he was going to kill him tonight. But he doesn't know, he doesn't know."

Skipping, I rounded the table, gathered five assorted plates, put them down in a circle on the ground, then sat on my rock and peeled the potatoes.

"I'll be ready to go tomorrow," I said as the

peels wound in spirals at my feet.

Suddenly the leather ferns rattled and James James walked into view. He was smiling. The woods people certainly had had a good day today.

Mom invited him to the celebration by simply sweeping her arms out over the feast and gesturing for him to sit down.

"Thank you," he said, and sat.

"Mom has a wonderful new job," I told him.

"Congratulations," he said with some sadness in his voice.

"You're a beautiful bird."

I would swear James James blushed as he looked at Mom, then he saw she was eating a raw bean and could not have spoken. Quick as a weasel's, his eyes scanned the camp, fell on Sherlock Holmes, and stayed there.

He grinned. "Where did you get him, Liza K.?" I thought I detected a little bit of disappointment in his voice.

"He's a woods person," I said.

"Homeless?" James James asked.

"If you call a free bird homeless."

With a warm smile James James offered the parrot his wrist. The bird stepped on it and they tonight. Pack up all your things."

"Tonight?" I cried. This was a crushing disappointment.

"Tonight," she answered. "A woman called the diner today and asked if you were home. Peggy answered. She said she must be a social worker. The woman wanted to know where to find you. The rumor is you hobnob with the woods people."

"What's wrong with that?" I said.

"They're not fit company for a young girl," she answered, as if using someone else's words. But to my astonishment she seemed to mean them.

"Mom," I cried, "what are you saying? You're talking about James James, Priscilla, and Caruso. Mom, they're the gentlest people we have ever known—you and I." She did not look at me.

"I have taken a room in a motel." She seemed so unlike herself, I wondered if my father was back.

"Please, no, Mom. Let me stay here—at least tonight."

"No," she said, and picked up a blouse to pack. "We must go. I want you out of here before we're caught."

"Please. I've got to see Dajun before I go."

She spun around to say no again just as Sherlock Holmes flew from the oak tree to my shoulder.

"Want to go out?" said the big, foot-tall parrot.

Mom blinked, and glanced from the bird to me and back to the bird. Then, unable to help herself, she smiled. Sherlock Holmes hung upside down from my shirt and eyed her.

"Well, thanks a lot," he said. The tension flowed out of Mom.

"Okay," she said. "You'll be all right for another night. We'll stay. I had planned to give a farewell party until Peggy told me about that call. It makes me very nervous. Someone is tracking you down."

"No, no," I said, recalling the map room conversation. "I know who made that call." I told her about Ms. Clara Lee Dade and the maps and how I blurted out the diner for an address.

"I know it was Ms. Dade calling," I said. "Who else would think the diner's my home? She's interested in Gumbo Limbo Hammock. I'm afraid she wants to see it." Mom listened, seemed to feel better, then slipped her arm around me and gave me a squeeze. Sherlock flew to the tent pole.

"Where did you get the parrot?" she asked. "He's wonderful."

"He must be a pet who got away. But now he lives in Gumbo Limbo Hammock with the homeless." Mom tousled my hair and walked up to the parrot.

"I like you, pretty bird," she said. Sherlock Holmes bowed and lifted his silver-tipped gray feathers to show them off to her, then flew to my shoulder and clucked gently to me.

"He's my detective," I said. "He gave me the missing clue to Dajun's whereabouts."

"He did? Where is he?" she asked.

"I can't tell you yet."

"Please do," Mom said. "I want to thank him. In a roundabout way Dajun's responsible for my getting the job." She took her backpack down from a hook.

"He is?" I said in astonishment. "How could he be?"

"It's all due to the salty water you found while searching for him," she answered. "I told the owner of the diner about the salt in the La Playa drinking water and suggested he use bottled water for the sake of the elderly. He made a few phone calls, found I was right, and—guess what he said."

"'You have the job.'"

"Better than that—two jobs." We smiled at each other.

"He also said," Mom went on, "that my professor at school had highly recommended me." I was so happy for her I clapped, although I was not quite so happy for myself. I didn't want to leave the hammock—ever—but I didn't want to leave my mother either. I wished we could both stay right here in the woods.

That, I knew now, was impossible, so I took down my backpack and began folding my clothes.

"Liza K.," Mom said. "do you realize we can stop being afraid? I have a good job and we'll have a nice home." I straightened up and stared at her, thinking many thoughts.

She opened her string bag and took out not just the daily container of soup and biscuits, but a large steak, a sack of potatoes, a bag of green beans, avocados, oranges, mangoes, and papayas.

"With this feast," she said, "we celebrate. Go find James James, Caruso, and Priscilla."

"I haven't seen anyone all day but Priscilla," I

said. "I think they're busy." I looked at the alarm clock. It was six thirty. One half hour to go. I left Mom packing her clothes and crept to the water's edge to watch Travis. If he was going to shoot Dajun, I would scream bloody murder and make him miss.

To my surprise Travis put his binoculars in their case and turned toward the trail. I couldn't believe it. Was he actually leaving? I closed my eyes and opened them. He had disappeared into the jungle. Absentmindedly I picked a flower and chewed its stem. I breathed shallow breaths. Then I heard Travis's car engine start, turn over, and move off, growing fainter and fainter. He was gone. I ran back to the tent.

"Mom," I said, my heart thumping a farewell fanfare to the alligator hunter, "Travis doesn't know where Dajun is. I thought he did. I thought he was going to kill him tonight. But he doesn't know, he doesn't know."

Skipping, I rounded the table, gathered five assorted plates, put them down in a circle on the ground, then sat on my rock and peeled the potatoes.

"I'll be ready to go tomorrow," I said as the

peels wound in spirals at my feet.

Suddenly the leather ferns rattled and James James walked into view. He was smiling. The woods people certainly had had a good day today.

Mom invited him to the celebration by simply sweeping her arms out over the feast and gesturing for him to sit down.

"Thank you," he said, and sat.

"Mom has a wonderful new job," I told him.

"Congratulations," he said with some sadness in his voice.

"You're a beautiful bird."

I would swear James James blushed as he looked at Mom, then he saw she was eating a raw bean and could not have spoken. Quick as a weasel's, his eyes scanned the camp, fell on Sherlock Holmes, and stayed there.

He grinned. "Where did you get him, Liza K.?" I thought I detected a little bit of disappointment in his voice.

"He's a woods person," I said.

"Homeless?" James James asked.

"If you call a free bird homeless."

With a warm smile James James offered the parrot his wrist. The bird stepped on it and they rubbed beak and nose. James James knew about parrots as he did about all of nature. He talked to the bird in soft clucks and whistles.

"Hello, Jean," the parrot said distinctly. "Want to go out?"

James James threw back his head and laughed.

"Got a name for him?"

"Sherlock Holmes."

"Why Sherlock Holmes?" he said, then whipped around and looked at me. "Where's Dajun?"

"I'll tell you when I've seen him."

"Give me a hint?"

"No," I answered.

I waited for him to beg me, but he did not. Instead he stroked the parrot's beak with a crooked forefinger and turned to Mom. Energetically he began telling her which of the canals that drained Silver City could be closed and which could not.

"But"—he paused—"there is one more thing. We can't close the canal over here until we know where the PCP is coming from. We don't want it seeping back into the ground."

"Any clues?"

"Yes. A kid from the condos told us some men

wash containers in the canal just north of where the fish died. I tested the water where they worked. It was heavily contaminated with PCP."

I was listening.

"Sweeney? I asked. "His plant's along the canal."

"I hope not," he said. "Have you seen Caruso this evening?" I sucked in my breath.

"He's probably singing," I answered, then counted hours and breathed again. The timing was wrong for Caruso and Beef Bones to be guilty.

At last the sun went down. The clouds turned pink, red, and turquoise blue. Then it was night. I left James James talking to Mom about water and municipal wells and slipped off to Gumbo Limbo Hole.

At Dajun's beach I climbed a tree that I had selected right after Sherlock Holmes had told me where Dajun was. From its second limb I could see the beach. Once more I waited, but not for long.

The water parted without a sound. An oval back, keeled with scutes, rose silently into view. There was not a gurgle, not a splash as Dajun's head appeared, water pouring off it like a surfacing submarine. He came ashore and climbed swiftly up the beach. A dark shadow, he lowered himself on the sun-warmed sand and let the heat seep into his cold body. I was right. Dajun was hiding under the water all day and coming out at night. He had reversed normal alligator behavior to keep from being killed.

"Hello," I whispered. "I'm so glad to see you."

After a long wait, the magnificent old dragon returned to the water, plowed some bladderwort weeds into the reeds, and came back with a garfish in his mouth. He smashed it with his lip-less mouth, then tilted his head back. Gravity carried the food to his belly. Alligators can't swallow.

"I knew you had to be here," I said. "There are no weeds in the hole. The fish are multiplying and the water is clear—almost. There are a few batches of blue-green algae you'll have to remove.

"You were down in the pit during the day, weren't you? Down where it is so cold you didn't have to breathe as often.

"You changed into a night 'gator. That's where you went."

I stayed in the tree until the moon came up and I could vaguely see the huge scutes, the great grinning mouth, and the popped eyes; then I climbed down and went home.

It was quite late. James James was gone, Mom was asleep, and Priscilla's, Caruso's, and my raw steaks were sitting in the candlelight on the table. Caruso must be still singing, but it would be nice to wake up Priscilla and have a party. I wondered if I should.

Yes, Priscilla was the dragon's poet, and whether she wrote down her poems or not, she should be the first to know that Dajun was safe. I cooked our steaks and, taking the candle, made my way to the gumbo limbo grove. Priscilla was at her desk, arms folded upon it, her candle burning. She was watching the bats maneuver through the tree limbs in the moonlight.

"Priscilla," I whispered. "Mom had a party. Why didn't you go?"

"Liza K.?" she answered fearfully. "Is that you?"

"Yes, it's me."

"Oh, Liza K., come into my house." I stepped over an imaginary line and presented her with the steak and fruit.

"Just place them over there," she said, pointing to the stump but also reaching out for them. "I'm really not hungry."

"Neither am I." I sat beside her and picked up

a knife. Hungrily we both ate.

"Are you writing poems?" I asked.

"Not since Dajun disappeared." This was what I wanted to hear. That's why her notebook was empty. She couldn't write without Dajun.

"Well, then, you can start again," I said. "Dajun is on his beach right now. I found him. He hides by day and comes out at night."

Holding her breath Priscilla got to her feet.

"Show me," she said, taking my hand.

Together we made our way to the beach, parted the trees that surrounded it, and looked down on the huge old Dajun basking in the moonlight warming himself as best he could on the sun-heated sand. He saw us, arose on his short legs, and pushed off into the water. No ripples or sound marked his departure. Presently we heard a loud splash and a slamming of teeth—twenty-eight to thirty in the lower jaw, thirty to forty in the upper jaw. A bird screeched and the water churned. The big 'gator rolled with his prey.

"Dear fellow," Priscilla said and turned away. "We must leave him to his privacy." She gave me an icy hand, and I led the way home on a foot path of moonlight.

"Will you make up more poems now?" I asked.

She squeezed my hand.

"If I can."

"What do you mean, if you can? Dajun is here."

"A social worker found me after you left. I was putting up hummingbird bottles in the field. I told her I knew you and your Mom, but that didn't help. She's coming to take me to the shelter."

I did not know what to say. Perhaps Priscilla could be helped like my father. Perhaps someone could talk to her about her fear of walls until she became peaceful and could live indoors in a comfortable apartment. Mom thinks that can happen. As far as I was concerned, she was wonderful just as she was.

"I'm glad Dajun's all right," she said, and sat down on her wicker chair bed.

"What will you do when the social worker comes to get you, Priscilla?" I asked.

"I'll do just what Dajun did. I'll turn into a night person." She patted my hand. "Liza K.," she said softly, "how did you know Dajun was up at night?"

"A parrot told me," I said. "He not only mimicked James James mimicking Dajun's roar, but he said, 'night, night.'" I chuckled. Priscilla smiled.

"I don't think he knew what he was saying," I went on. "But I did."

"I'm ready to sleep," she said, and I picked up the plates and tiptoed away.

As I walked home, stepping on silver spots of moonlight, I thought of how frightened Priscilla would be in a place with four walls, a ceiling, and a floor. I hoped someone would hold her hand and maybe keep her wicker chair outside in case she became panic-stricken. Anyone who has been hurt can understand Priscilla. I wiped my eyes and ran in and out of the magnificent trees.

Inside the yellow tent I listened for a long time to the frogs and crickets and thought about Priscilla, Dajun, and incredible Gumbo Limbo Hammock. Somehow all three must survive.

At five A.M., while it was still dark as night, I climbed the oak. An enormous shadow slid down the alligator beach and disappeared into Gumbo Limbo Hole.

Two hours later the sun came up. Travis arrived on the beach. Singing smugly to myself, I climbed down the tree.

Now to find where Dajun stayed by daylight. The mystery was not completely solved.

9
Resolved

The water for oatmeal had just begun to boil when James James came around the leather fern.

"Hey," he said stopping beside the stove. "I didn't sleep all night trying to figure out where Dajun is. I give up. Where is he?"

"In Gumbo Limbo Hole."

"Come on," he said. "We've looked there."

"Not down in the lake pit," I said.

"I sure have. Just yesterday I saw down to the bottom—down to the green algae on the rocks and logs. There was no alligator there. I think you're mistaken."

"I saw him on his beach last night," I said, grinning victoriously.

"You did?" James James was flabbergasted.

"He's very smart," I said. "He stays under the water all day and comes ashore after dark." The surprise lines on James James's face ironed out as he considered what I had said.

"Priscilla said she read somewhere that an alligator can hold its breath for five hours."

"That's rare," James James said. "And that's only five hours. He still has to come up to breathe, and when he does—Travis shoots him."

"Well, he didn't; and he's alive. I saw him."

"I'm going to check it out," he said and climbed the oak. I turned off the stove and climbed after him.

The limb I usually sit on was too small to hold us both, so I stood below James James on another limb. I couldn't see as well, but I didn't need to.

"See him?" I asked.

"No," he answered. "The water's crystal clear. I don't see anything but fish all the way to the bottom."

"To the bottom of the deep hole in the middle?"

"To the bottom of the deep hole," he answered. "There's just green algae down there as I said."

"Green algae," I asked, "or blue-green?"

"Green."

"Not the pollution algae?"

"Green," he insisted. "There's no pollution here, you know that. And now I know why. I saw a geological study of this area. There's a ridge of sand just north of Gumbo Limbo Hammock. The rain picks up the surface pollutants from farms, businesses, and homes north of that, hits the ridge, and flows east toward the Big Cypress Preserve. The condo wells don't draw on our aquifer, so we sit on a bubble of fresh water all our own. The solution pit and hole are as pure as sunshine. I tested them."

"Well," I said, thinking about the land, "I can believe that. But I also believe Dajun's here."

"He isn't," James James insisted. "I'm looking in the pit."

"Let me look," I said, perplexed. James James eased himself down and I climbed up. The sunlight was now shining brightly, and the long needles of the slash pines were a sea of silver sabers. The royal palm leaves were chiming and Gumbo Limbo Hole was clear as glass. I leaned far out. James James was right. Only the good green algae covered the rocks at the bottom of the deep hole. There was no alligator.

Green algae, I said to myself. I could hear a bell ringing but again, I couldn't find a door to open. Green algae.

"Let me look again," James James said, and we switched places.

"I know Dajun's there," I insisted. "Priscilla and I both saw him last night. What's going on?"

"I don't know," he said. "There are no underwater caves for him to hide in. I checked that out on the geology map."

Puzzled, we climbed down. Sherlock Holmes passed us as he flew into a strangler fig tree ladened with seeds.

"Your Mom doesn't have to bring soup home for him," James James said. "There's parrot food galore here. No wonder he left home." The parrot's bright red tail caught James James's eye.

"And by the way," he said, "Sherlock Holmes has made a liar of me. Caruso is right. There *is* a bird with bright-red tail feathers in southern Florida." We laughed. I swung from the lowest limb and dropped to the ground.

Mom was up and packing the last of her

clothes. She kissed me good morning.

"Hello, James James," she said. "Was Sherlock Holmes right? Did he tell Liza K. where Dajun was?"

"Not quite," he answered. "We haven't quite solved the mystery."

"He comes up on land at night when that alligator hunter is gone," I said. "So he's right there in Gumbo Limbo Hole."

"But he also isn't in the hole," James James said.

I lit the flame under the oatmeal again—and thought about the blue-green algae.

"You said you tested our water, James James?" I asked. "And you didn't find any pollutants in it?"

"That's right." He looked at his watch. "Whoops, I've got to go," he said. "I'll help you find Dajun later. He's stayed hidden this long—he's not likely to make an appearance while Travis is here today. Early this morning I met a scientist from the Environmental Protection Agency walking along the canal. He's traced the PCP to a spot below Sweeney's plant. He wants to meet with me and the director in about ten minutes." He looked at me. I looked at him.

"Caruso had nothing to do with it," I said in a firm voice. He nodded, but also frowned.

"The penalty is a huge fine."

"James James," Mom said packing the tin cups, "do you by any chance have a job?" Her eyes twinkled.

"Heavens, no," he answered. "I'm just donating my services."

"But you're working as hard as the director. You should ask for a consultant's fee."

"I'm just fine," he said, and walked off through the woods, his stride a little quicker than was usual. As he passed the coco plum, a cloud of butterflies flew up.

"Mom," I said. "A hatch." Picking up my binoculars, I chased after them to identify them. I haven't caught adult butterflies since I read in my field guide that lepidopterists identify butterflies through binoculars just like bird watchers do.

When I returned, without having seen even one butterfly close enough to know what it was, Mom was putting her pack on her back. "Liza K.," she said, "please be ready to leave when I come back this afternoon."

I didn't want to promise. I had found Dajun,

but I hadn't found Dajun. Furthermore, James James had to lure him into the solution pit. That might take a long time.

I was washing the dishes when Caruso came home. He looked tired. His eyelids were drooping and his clothes mussed.

"How did it go, Caruso?" I asked.

"How did what go?"

"Your concert."

"Yes. Yes. The concert. Very well. I was cheered and cheered. I took seventeen curtain calls. Fans carried me on their shoulders from one concert hall where I sang to the next. I'm very tired."

"Want some oatmeal?" I asked.

"Yes, I do," he said, and sat down. I served him some in a bowl.

"Mom and I will soon be leaving," I said. "Would you sing for me, Caruso? I've never heard you sing."

"I'd never sing here in the woods," he said. "Do you want them to find me and put me in that shelter with Mr. Burnster? Do you?"

"No, Caruso, I don't."

"Then don't ask me to sing." He turned his

back and ate the cereal.

"I found Dajun," I said. He spun around.

"You found him?" He smiled and then scowled. "What good does that do? He's still twelve feet long. He's still declared a dangerous individual, and Travis still has orders to shoot him." He glanced around nervously. "Where's James James?"

"He's checking the PCP. Somebody washed containers that had held wood preservative in the canal, and it killed lots of fish."

"Who would do that?" he asked.

"Would Sweeney?" I asked very softly.

He cocked his head to one side and thought. "I hope that's not what he's doing," he said. "I hope not. Beef Bones and I have been helping. We do wash cans in the canal."

"Did you know what had been in the cans you were washing?"

"No," he said honestly. "I was doing my job. What did you say the stuff was?"

"PCP."

"Is it bad?"

"It's bad," I answered.

"I think I did see those letters on the cans." His deep-set eyes peered at me.

"Does Sweeney know that?" I asked.

"Sweeney?" Caruso threw his hands up. "He doesn't even know how to spell his name."

"Good," I said. "Maybe they'll just give him a warning."

"Oh, Liza K." He sighed deeply. "That's terrible—poisons and all. Life's just gotten too complicated. I'm not leaving here again. I'm staying right here in these woods."

"But what about singing? You'll sing, won't you?"

"Of course I'll sing. I have to earn a living." I was glad to hear that.

"Where will you be singing tonight, Caruso?" If I was going to be in town in a motel, I might as well do something worthwhile.

"At the pier," he answered, putting his empty bowl in the soap pan. "I must go. I need to rest my voice for tonight. Thank you."

When he was gone, I climbed the oak and once more peered into that deep pit in the hole. The solution to the mystery had to be down in there. Again I saw only the green algae and the fish. And I saw Travis sitting in the willows waiting. "Stay down, old dragon, wherever you are," I whispered. "Stay down." Slowly I descended to the ground and began packing my books and caterpillar cages.

"Where are you going?"

I fairly jumped out of my skin, came to my senses, and laughed. Sherlock Holmes was back from the strangler fig.

"Where are you going?" he asked.

"None of your business," I replied, smiling sadly. Did he know I was leaving, or was it just chance that he said the right thing at the right time? I crooked my arm and held it up, and he flew to it and walked to my shoulder.

"Hello, pretty girl," he said, moving his throat feathers.

"Oh, hush," I said, smirking delightedly. He did say such appropriate things that I could not help but think he knew what he was saying.

It didn't take me long to pack. I had very few clothes, mostly bugs and books. I should have rolled up the sleeping bags and struck the tent, but I wasn't going to leave Gumbo Limbo Hammock until I was sure Dajun was safe.

Around noon Travis gave up his search. I guess he figured the best time to get a good shot at an alligator is in the morning, when it comes ashore to bask in the sun. He was right, except for this one smart fellow. But one of these days, maybe tonight, Travis was going to stay after dark—and that would be fatal.

Having packed, I climbed to the treetop once again. I still thought the answer was down in the water. You have to be persistent with nature. She gives up her secrets reluctantly. I searched the lake, its shallow and deep water, the reeds, the saw grass, the flags—everything.

"James James is wrong," I said aloud. "Some fertilizer or some pollutant *is* getting into Gumbo Limbo Hole. That *is* blue-green algae in the water below the royal palm."

Climbing swiftly to the ground, I ran to the palm to look closer at the blob of alga.

"Good afternoon."

I looked up to greet Sherlock Holmes, but there stood Ms. Clara Lee Dade from the county building.

"Oh, hello," I stammered, horrified to see her. I had led Ms. Dade to Gumbo Limbo Hammock and to the end of life in the woods for James James, Priscilla, and Caruso.

"This hammock is remarkable," she said, looking up at the leaves. "I've already found forty different trees that grow in hammocks. And the birds—I saw a yellow-billed cuckoo."

What should I do with Ms. Dade? I couldn't send her to the golf course or the canals, so I just stood still and looked at her.

"The lake is remarkable, too," she went on. "It's alive with gambusia fish, bass, and shiners. Lots of healthy good fish.

"And I've found orchids that I haven't seen since the orchid growers raided our hammocks and took almost all the wild ones away. This is a wonderful place—extraordinary." She lifted her binoculars and peered into the woods.

"Look at that mahogany," she said. My heart thumped. Caruso's home was there. What had I done to my friends of the woods? I had brought this woman to destroy them, that's what I had done.

"That tree must be three or four hundred years old," she said in wonderment. "This place is unbelievable."

"Yes, it is," I agreed, and desperately tried to think how to divert her. "Yes it is." By now I realized what a good naturalist she was. I had one chance.

"It should be saved," I blurted out. "Just as it is. It's a national treasure."

Ms. Dade lowered her binoculars.

"You're right," she said. "That's exactly why I'm here. This hammock should be saved." Her face was softened by a lovely smile. Then I remembered she worked for the county.

"No picnic tables and benches," I said. "Just nature."

"Just nature," she answered. "Yes, just nature. And I know exactly how to keep it that way. I inquired from the railroad trust. It can be bought and I know who will buy it."

"Who?" I asked eagerly.

"A group of men who have formed a wildlife foundation. They have been searching for one last undefiled hammock in southern Florida to preserve. They will study it as a model and return vanished plants and animals to the ravaged hammocks.

"I can tell you that the president will shout in joy when I bring him here." She looked around. I just stood there gaping at her—disbelieving and believing.

"But this hammock must have a caretaker to

protect it from vandals," she went on.

"That's me." I turned around to see James James leaning on a gumbo limbo tree behind us. He introduced himself to Ms. Dade.

"And why you?" she asked perkily.

"Because I'm a very good naturalist and I love this hammock. I would even defend that mosquito on your arm against a swat." He smiled. James James has a very infectious smile, and Ms. Dade caught it. She smiled, too.

"Could you meet with me and my friends tomorrow?" she asked James James.

"Indeed I could," he replied. "But let me give you a tour of the wonders before you talk to your friends."

As they walked off I got down on my belly and wiggled to the water's edge.

"Blue-green algae, meow," I said cheering. "Hello, Dajun."

The big old reptile was lying on the bottom in the sun growing green algae on his back like all the other underwater objects. The brown color of his skin shone through the green alga and made it look blue-green. And he was calmly breathing in a somewhat unusual way. Instead of poking both his eyes and his nose above the water, a sight that is easy for a human to recognize as an alligator, he was lying with just his nostrils out, as alligators do in cold weather. And he had poked his nostrils up among the dark round seeds of the royal palm that were floating all around him. His two nostrils looked exactly like the palm seeds. Nobody, but nobody, would have known those black buttons and that mess of green was Dajun.

"You're a clever one," I said to our dragon. "Green algae on your dark skin looks blue-green. I thought you were the beginning of the death of Gumbo Limbo Hole. You're not. You're just old Dajun—and I love you."

I scrambled to my feet, hurried to the oak, and climbed it again to make sure the two masses of algae I had seen were both Dajun. There was no blob in the pit now, just under the palm. The masses were one and the same. I just hadn't noticed that they moved.

And then it occurred to me—if Gumbo Limbo Hammock was made a nature preserve, Dajun must not be killed. He was the most important preservationist in the whole environment. It would not be hard to convince Ms. Dade of that.

I stayed up in the oak for a long time watching butterflies and singing to myself. In the late afternoon James James returned without Ms. Dade, and I scrambled down. He grabbed both my hands and spun me around in a square-dance swing.

"Liza K.," he said. "You've not only saved Gumbo Limbo Hammock. I have a job."

"From nine to five?" I gasped.

"No, from twelve A.M. around the clock to twelve A.M.," he said. "Ms. Dade wants a naturalist who will live in the woods and protect it twenty-four hours a day."

"But what about the foundation that is buying it? Maybe they don't want you."

"I asked her about that," James James said smiling. "The president and chairman of the board is her father." We grinned at each other, then danced again, improvising alligator polkas as we circled the oak tree.

Suddenly I stopped dancing. "James James," I said. "What will you do about Priscilla? Will she have to sleep in a four-walled room?"

"I talked about her with Ms. Dade," James James said. "She had already met Priscilla putting out her hummingbird feeders and was very impressed with her knowledge. But Priscilla needs help so that she can adjust to living indoors. She can't live here forever. She will work with the county social workers in her gumbo limbo home until she's ready to go."

I thought back to my last conversation with Priscilla. "So it wasn't a social worker who met her in the tomato field. It was Ms. Dade. I'll go tell her so she won't be frightened."

"I already have. Ms. Dade and I went by to see her," James James said. "She has agreed to try to love walls."

I did not know how anyone could possibly help Priscilla love walls—unless—unless, as it had for me, Gumbo Limbo Hammock had already worked its miracle and she was ready to leave.

"And will Caruso have to live in a shelter with Mr. Burnster?" I asked.

"As a matter of fact," he said, "Sweeney is going to give Beef Bones and him not only jobs, but lodging at his plant. He needs them as watchmen. I have just spoken to Caruso. He said he didn't know he was any good to anyone. He had given up."

"Was he pleased?"

"I really think he was," James James said.

I picked up my brush and ran it through my hair as I thought about Caruso. Then I changed the subject.

"Is Sweeney guilty?" I asked.

"Yes, but out of ignorance." James James answered. "He won't be fined this time. He really didn't know what PCP was." We looked at each other and smiled.

"Are you all right?" Sherlock Holmes flew in.

"Yes," I answered, and held up my arm. He alighted on it and walked to my shoulder. I rubbed his beak gently with my nose. He lifted his feathers affectionately.

"You're wonderful," I said.

"You're wonderful," he repeated. James James cocked his head and listened.

"Say that again, Liza K."

"You're wonderful," I said.

"You're wonderful," said the parrot.

"Liza K.," James James said thoughtfully, rubbing his chin. "I think you'll have to take Sherlock Holmes with you.

"Really?" I cried excitedly. "Really?"

"Scientists have discovered that wild parrots imitate the voices of their mates. It's part of bonding. That's why they imitate people when they are in captivity."

"You mean I'm his mate?"

"Or a sister or brother," James James said. "Whatever your relationship, you now have a contract with him."

"A contract?"

"A social contract. You must not break it by leaving him here. He would not do well."

"I won't, I won't," I said.

"I won't, I won't," Sherlock Holmes repeated. James James and I laughed and I knew he was right. I must keep faith with the bird.

Dropping to my knees, I began to strike the tent. "I'd better get ready to go," I said, pulling up the stakes. James James put them in their bag.

"I'll be in town tonight," I said.

"So I hear," he said sadly. "I'll miss you—terribly." Tears burned behind my eyes. I watched the tent collapse. It billowed, then fluttered to the ground, a crumpled castle.

"I think I'll go to Caruso's concert when I'm in town tonight," I said. "I've never heard him sing, and I want to very much."

James James stopped stuffing the tent into its bag.

146 〜〜

"I don't think you want to go to Caruso's concert, Liza K.," he said softly. I looked up into his face and read what was there.

"Oh," I said, recalling Priscilla's empty notebook. "Oh, I guess I don't."

As I rolled up the tent rain flap, James James reached into his pocket and took out a piece of notebook paper.

"Priscilla gave me this," he said. "She wanted me to read it to you." He lifted his head. "'We love the things we love for what they are.'"

I just stood there as the simple words bloomed like a flower within me.

"Why, that's beautiful," I said, smiling with happiness. "Priscilla *is* a poet. She writes wonderful poetry. She really does." James James put the paper in his pocket and laid his hand gently on my shoulder. I looked up at him.

"'We love the things we love for what they are,'" he recited, then added softly, "by Robert Frost."

Walking slowly to the oak I leaned the tent pack against it. After a moment I turned around.

"Priscilla *reads* wonderful poets," I said and smiled.

I couldn't think of anything more to say to

James James. Robert Frost's words and my friends of Gumbo Limbo Hammock were in my thoughts. James James was quiet, too. He put the slip of paper back into his pocket. For several minutes we stood in silence in the spangled shade, looking at nothing in particular.

"James James," I finally said. "If you go to the royal palm and look down in the water, you'll see a mass of blue-green algae under the floating palm seeds."

His eyes snapped alive. "I know what you're going to say. Is it really?"

"Really."

He laughed as if he had just been let in on the magic secrets of a mighty magician. Then, taking to his toes, he ran full speed to the hole.

"Dajun!" I heard him cry. "You old conjurer you. You're great. Hang in there, old man. We're all going to make it together."

"The whole wide world of us," I added, squeezing my eyes tightly shut and pressing my fingers over the three-inch smile on my face.

Mom would be coming for me soon.